T0131772

Brady gripped Kylie's hand and pulled her to a stop. He was pensive as he stared down at her. Clearly, something was on his mind, and Kylie wondered if this was all a little too much, too fast for him—Franny's heart attack, Kylie admitting her feelings...her inability to be this close to him without aching to kiss him.

Gingerly, he plucked something from her hair. "Snowflake."

"Brady, I—"

He leaned in to kiss her, stealing her words as his lips performed their own version of magic. It took him a moment to pull away. "I'm sorry. It was just seeing you out here, snow all around us, it reminded me of another time."

Several of the people passing by had stopped to watch the children. There was something about snow in a place like a movie theater that made kids want to be silly. Kylie knew because this wasn't the first time she and Brady had been outside a movie theater, snow in the air, only that time school had been canceled and there was six inches on the ground. They'd just started whatever they were starting, and so when he came by her house and said he was taking her to a movie, she didn't argue. She grinned ear to ear, grabbed her coat, and followed him to his truck. At the time, she would have followed him anywhere.

"I know. I was thinking about the same thing," she said. "It was the moment I knew you wanted more than friendship."

Brady laughed loudly, the sound rumbling from his chest to hers. "Make no mistake, sweetheart. I never had my sights on friendship." His expression turned serious. "I think I loved you the moment I met you..."

Books by Melissa West

Hamilton Stables

RACING HEARTS
WILD HEARTS
SILENT HEARTS

The Littleton Brothers

FIGHTING LOVE
CHASING LOVE
MERRILY IN LOVE

Published by Kensington Publishing Corporation

MERRILY IN LOVE

Melissa West

LYRICAL SHINE
Kensington Publishing Corp.
www.kensingtonbooks.com

LYRICAL SHINE BOOKS are published by

Kensington Publishing Corp.
119 West 40th Street
New York, NY 10018

All Kensington titles, imprints, and distributed lines are available at special quantity discounts for bulk purchases for sales promotion, premiums, fund-raising, educational, or institutional use.

Special book excerpts or customized printings can also be created to fit specific needs. For details, write or phone the office of the Kensington Sales Manager: Kensington Publishing Corp., 119 West 40th Street, New York, NY 10018. Attn. Sales Department. Phone: 1-800-221-2647.

Lyrical Shine and Lyrical Shine logo Reg. U.S. Pat. & TM Off.

First Electronic Edition: November 2017
eISBN-13: 978-1-60183-992-3
eISBN-10: 1-60183-992-8

First Print Edition: November 2017
ISBN-13: 978-1-60183-993-0
ISBN-10: 1-60183-993-6

Printed in the United States of America

For my sweet Lainey, who has always loved Christmas.

Acknowledgments

Thank you so much to God for helping me complete this book! It was a tough journey, but I am so thankful I pushed on to create these characters and tell their story.

I could not go about my day without the support, humor, and love of my amazing family. Thank you to Jason for showing me love on a continuous basis and to my two beautiful daughters for humbling me day after day.

Thank you to my mom and dad for buying multiple copies of every book I write and asking me to sign them. You are such wonderful parents.

Lastly, thank you to the team at Kensington for helping shape this book, and to you, the reader for taking time out of your day to meet my characters. I so appreciate you!

Chapter 1

The bell dinged from Southern Dive's door, and immediately, Brady Littleton's dude intuition perked up. He set down the black pen he'd been tapping against the packing slip from that morning's delivery and peered over. A slow smile curled his lips at the sight of the blonde walking through the door. Nice rack, tan skin, a look that said she knew her way around a boat…and a man. Maybe a water skier, maybe a diver.

Maybe someone interested in a certain single business owner.

The woman was one of many to catch Brady's eye this week, all in an effort to get his mind off the approaching date. Like always, the holidays reminded him of the single time in his life that he'd been happy, truly happy…and how it had all disappeared.

Thankfully, the shop was busy for fall, which helped keep his mind off the past and focused on the present and future. Online orders had picked up, and that coupled with increased foot traffic in the store, and Brady suspected Southern Dive would have its busiest holiday season ever.

Take today. It was two o'clock on a Thursday afternoon, and so far, more people had shopped in Southern Dive than all of last week. Brady made a mental note to ask his brother, Charlie, if he'd advertised on social media or used his giant Instagram following to push a sale. His past as a corporate sales analyst made it hard for him to ignore sales changes like these. He liked to track trends, uncover the whys, and then implement policy that would help those sales remain consistent.

But that would be work for later tonight, when Brady was alone in his house, watching some game he didn't care about, a to-go box on the table because he hated making dinner for one. For now, Brady had his sights on other things. Specifically, the leggy blonde. Perhaps tonight he could order dinner for two.

He walked around the hand-built wooden counter against the left-hand wall of the shop and started toward the blonde. She wore black leggings, a long, red plaid shirt that she'd rolled to her elbows, and brown duck boots unlaced at the top. Her face glowed in a way that hinted at light makeup, and as he neared, he caught the telltale shine on her lips from lip gloss.

God, he loved lip gloss. It had a wet, flirty vibe to it that lipstick couldn't match. A put-together woman with goals and expectations wore lipstick. He knew. He'd met many of those kinds of women back in his corporate days, and while there was nothing wrong with put-together, he preferred fun and carefree. And a fun, carefree woman wore lip gloss.

"Looking for something in particular?" he asked, flashing a crooked grin. It was a trademark move, one that had served him well in his twenty-nine years.

The blonde paused midway to a wetsuit and glanced over. She blinked, taking him in, then flashed her own smile, and he knew he had her.

Brady understood his strengths, and his face had always been one of them.

"Nice shirt," she said, eyeing his T-shirt.

Charlie had started designing T-shirts a year before, and now they received as many orders for his classic designs as anything else. Today, Brady sported a shirt that read: JUST BREATHIN', DRINKIN' & FISHIN'.

The blonde scanned the shop before focusing back on Brady, her smile returning like she couldn't help it if she tried. Yeah, he definitely had her. "Do you sell those here?"

"In fact, we do. Is this for you or a friend?" Brady directed her over to the shelf of T-shirts, hundreds of then tucked into tiny cubbies. They had forty different designs on the floor, more still in the stockroom in the back. "A boyfriend, maybe?" He winked, and her cheeks flushed.

"No boyfriend. I'm shopping for a birthday present for my dad."

"In that case, I can help you."

She grinned wider, settling into their flirtation. "So you couldn't help me if I were here for a boyfriend?"

A car door closed outside, and Brady suspected at least one of his brothers was there to go over their plans for an expansion. A plan Brady had been working on for months and had finally come to fruition, thanks to Ms. Franny May's supposed retirement.

"I'd help, but not so personally. And I probably wouldn't offer you a buy one get one fifty percent off deal so you could get this one for yourself."

He took out a long-sleeve Southern Dive shirt, bright pink with white letters. It was a popular one for ladies who came through the shop. "You know, so you can remember me when you're wearing it."

She took a step toward him and braced herself against the shelf as she looked up at him. "I don't think I'll need anything to help me remember you, but I'd love to give you my number so you can be sure to remember me."

Brady bit his lip and stared at the blonde, yet another move that never failed him, and pulled his phone from his back pocket. "What's your name, sweetheart?"

"Brantley."

He froze, his phone's screen still dark, as the name settled uncomfortably in his mind. Brady, Brantley. The names were so similar, and with his dark blond hair and her light blond hair, people could make the assumption that they were siblings. Like brother and sister. Shit, now he'd pictured her as his sister. This wasn't going to work at all.

"859-348-5951."

Charlie came in at that moment, followed by his other brother, Zac, and Brady had his save. He quickly typed in the number he had no intention of calling. "Feel free to take your time. Register's right up there." He pointed to the front of the store. "Gotta catch up with my brothers, but give me a yell if you need anything." He winked, because that was his thing, and she grinned back.

"I'll be sure to do that."

A few more customers came in, creating a much-needed distraction so he could get to the counter and try to talk to his brothers.

"Meet a new one?" Charlie asked as he set down his laptop, opened it up, and began checking his various social media accounts. He was the creative one out of the three brothers and had generously agreed to carry his best-selling T-shirt line at the shop instead of on his own. It was a selfless act, something common with Charlie.

"New shirt?" Brady asked him, hoping to avoid the conversation about the blonde and the reason why Brady wouldn't—*couldn't*—call her.

Charlie glanced down at his long-sleeve gray shirt, likely forgetting what he'd put on that morning. It had a skeletal horse with wings in the center. Nothing fancy. He paired the shirt with cargo shorts and flip-flops, because Charlie would rather get frostbite than switch from his beach wear to winter wear. A part of him would always live on some island in the Keys, not a care in the world.

"One of my suppliers sent it for me to test out," Charlie said. "Now, don't change the subject. Thought I saw you flirting with that lady, then all of a sudden you freaked out. Again."

"Yeah, Charlie's right. This is becoming a trend," Zac, his other brother, said, chiming in now. Like Brady, he wore one of Charlie's designs, this one a fish trapped in a net, and jeans. His light brown hair stuck off his head in spikes. Brady contemplated calling out his hair gel obsession, but that would only give his brothers more motivation to harass him.

"What is it this time?" Charlie asked, refusing to let it go. "Split ends?"

"What? No, it's not split ends." Brady busied himself with a water bottle and a cap that refused to unscrew. He set the bottle down before he slammed it in aggravation, which confirmed to his brothers that something was up.

And something was up. Majorly up. Brady just didn't know what had caused it. Sure, this time of year always brought on dark thoughts, but this was more than all that emotional crap.

It all started with a dream. A horrible dream. The kind of dream that felt an awful lot like happiness, which were always the worst kind. And those types of horrible dreams always featured the same person.

After that, Brady couldn't get his brain to stop thinking about her, couldn't make himself think about another woman. So instead of enjoying a woman the way a man should enjoy her, the way she deserved to be enjoyed, every woman he met left his world as abruptly as she entered it.

Sure, he was nitpicky at times, but he was a few months away from turning thirty, and now wasn't the time to waste on useless women. He had to focus on his family and their business if he hoped to win back his family's trust and respect.

"If not her hair, then what?" Zac asked.

Brady shook his head. "You're annoying as all hell, you know that?"

"Yeah, well, you love me, so spill it. What's wrong with her?" He eyed the blonde, and Brady followed his gaze, only to catch her looking at him before glancing away.

The problem is she isn't Ky—

Not going there. Not at all going there. And if he couldn't admit the truth, he'd have to offer up the next closest thing.

"Her name's Brantley."

Charlie stared at him. "And...?"

"Brantley. Like Brady. It's like freaking sibling names or something."

"Did you just say that our names sound like sibling names?"

Shit.

Brady turned around to find Brantley standing at the register, two shirts and a pullover in hand. She made good choices, which impressed Brady until he thought of her name again and he cringed.

"Heard that did you?" he asked with a laugh, hoping if he laughed it off she wouldn't be too upset. Then again, what did he care? He had no intention of seeing her ever again, but he didn't want to give the shop or Charlie's shirts a bad rap.

"Let me guess? You're one of those guys who finds something wrong in every woman you meet, all because you have some age-old fixation on a woman you can't really have." She stared at Brady and both his brothers faced him, Charlie's eyebrows raised, and he seriously considered telling them to go to hell, but then that damn reputation thing and all.

"I..." Brady started, but before he could say anything else Charlie stepped up to help Brantley check out.

"Just these, then?" Charlie asked. He pushed Brady back, and Zac grabbed his shoulder and directed him toward the back.

"Hey, brother, need you to look at something in the stockroom."

Charlie bagged up Brantley's purchases, and slowly the guilt in Brady's chest spread. Why did he get himself into these messes?

The stockroom smelled like a combination of a basement and cleaning products. It was organized in row after row of metal shelves, each with different inventory stacked and labeled with item number, name, and inventory count. Brady implemented an inventory management system a few years ago, but he still preferred to keep a hand count of all stocked items.

"All right, new rule," Zac said, once they were safely inside the stockroom. "No hitting on women who come into the shop. You're going to screw over half our customers."

"I didn't screw her. I didn't even go out with her. She gave me her number, but then she said her name and..."

"And what?" Zac grinned, which said he and Charlie had talked about this little quirk of his and analyzed all the reasons Brady was this side of crazy.

"You heard me in there. There's no need to explain further."

"So you're ditching women because of their name now? What if that was your future wife back there?"

Brady cocked his head, because there was only one future wife for him, and she walked away a long damn time ago.

Relenting, Zac crossed his arms, but continued to watch his brother. Something a lot like concern crossed his face. "All right, so maybe not your future wife, but hell man, you can't just ask for a woman's number, then not call her."

Brady resisted the urge to roll his eyes. Zac had always been the good brother, the one to never step too far out of line, particularly when it came to women. Something told Brady that Zac raising a daughter had something to do with his weird need to be overly chivalrous, but he knew better than to suggest as much.

"Hey, at least I didn't sleep with her then not call."

Zac opened his mouth to argue, but closed it back and shook his head. "I'm not even going there. Just try to choose women who are not customers, okay?"

"Not a problem," Brady said, and he meant it. At this point, he wondered if he would ever find a woman who could interest him on any real level.

"Onto business," Zac said. "Have you set up that meeting with Franny yet?"

A rumbling sounded from outside, followed by a woman cursing, and they both glanced over to the back door.

"You hear that?"

Zac waved it off. "Yeah, probably Annie-Jean bringing in stuff to the bakery. I'll check with her in a second. Back to the question—have you set up the meeting with Franny?"

Ms. Franny May ran the Christmas shop next door to Southern Dive. She was long past retirement age, and it was no secret that she struggled to keep the business afloat. So when the Littleton brothers decided to expand, it made sense to reach out to Franny first. They hoped to buy her building, which Franny had owned since forever, and convert it into a shipping location for the shop. Maybe even add bait and tackle for local fishermen. They weren't sure what all they could do with it, but their store was becoming more and more retail and less and less dive lessons, so it made sense to get some extra space. And if all went as planned, Franny's Christmas shop would be theirs in no time.

"Meeting with her in half an hour, actually. You planning on joining?"

Zac shook his head. "Nah, you might be pond scum with women, but you're our numbers man. Plus, Franny's always liked you best."

Brady glanced at the door, hoping his brother wouldn't delve into why Franny had always liked him. Or how much time he'd spent at Franny's shop when he was a teenager. It wasn't a part of his past that he liked to discuss or even think about, which was why he'd put off the meeting for nearly a month. He didn't want to deal with all the questions that were sure to pop up from Franny—nor the questions he'd want to ask her about a certain goddaughter.

"Right. Well, I'm going to go check on Annie-Jean. You going out front?" Brady nodded. "Yeah, hopefully it's safe now."

Zac disappeared out the back door, and Brady turned around to grab some coffee before going to talk to Franny. He needed all the liquid courage he could get, and Franny would give him the side-eye if he showed up smelling like beer. Coffee would have to do.

He peeked out the storage room door to find the shop empty except for Charlie.

"You're safe to come out," Charlie called. "All victims of your attention have left the building."

"Funny," Brady said as he pushed out the door, a box of keychains and magnets in hand to replenish the depleted stock by the register.

"Well, she did tell me to tell you not to call her and to lose her number."

"Ah." Brady went to work putting keychains on their rightful hooks on the front of the counter. "Probably deserved that."

"Yeah." Charlie paused long enough that Brady looked up.

"What?"

"Nothing, it's just…"

"Just spill it."

"Have you talked to her recently?"

Brady laughed sarcastically. Even his brothers wouldn't use her name. "Recently? That suggests that I've talked to her at all since she left. Nah, man, she called a 'see ya' and never looked back."

"Right."

His eyes lifted to find his brother staring at him with the same pity he wore every time they talked about Brady's one and only serious girlfriend. "Take those sad puppy dog eyes elsewhere. I'm fine."

Charlie nodded slowly. "Sure you are. Hey, where are you going?"

"Gotta meeting with Franny," Brady answered, already across the store to the exit.

"Thought that wasn't for another half hour."

Brady flashed his brother a grin to cover up how uncomfortable he felt inside. "Some of us prefer to be early." The excuse was weak, but the alternative wasn't an option. Thinking about her was hard. Talking about her? Agonizing. Why put himself through that shit?

"You're avoiding the subject," Charlie called as Brady slipped outside.

Damn straight.

* * * *

Kylie Waters tucked her brown hair back behind her ears, leaned down to grab a box of ornaments, and immediately the wild curls fell back into her face.

"Geez Louise," she huffed, then shook her head to move the spiraling strands from her eyes, which they refused to do, because her hair cooperated with her about as much as her life these days. Hence her return to Crestler's Key in the first place.

She lifted the box up higher and glanced down at the next three boxes, all filled with ornaments like the first, all purchased on credit. A sinking feeling swallowed her heart for a moment, but Kylie reminded herself that this was why she was here—to help her godmother, Franny, with the shop. To fix things. Even if being back in her hometown felt like walking out in the sun when she was already burned.

The perfect blue sky stretched above her, not a cloud in sight, and the temperature held at sixty-two. Which was another one of Merrily Christmas's problems—shoppers didn't love buying Christmas stuff when it was warm outside. But it was November, and any week now the temps could drop down into the forties and stick there through December, where they would dip down again and stick. It was a matter of time, Kylie knew, but that didn't help the bottom line move into the green any faster.

She knocked on the back door to the shop and waited, but after another minute, when no one came, she figured Franny must have returned to sorting the other ornaments Kylie had brought inside.

"All right, box, I need you to stay together for another few seconds." She set the box on the ground, ripping one of the corners in the process. "Damn, cheap boxes." She opened the back door and propped it open with her foot, then bent down to grab the box. Another rip. Crap.

Edging inside the door, Kylie slowed her pace, careful not to squeeze the box or adjust her hold for fear that the bottom would fall out and all the ornaments would crash to the ground, where they were sure to break. Kylie's luck ran that way these days.

It all started with her losing her teaching job back in South Carolina due to budget cuts. Who needed art class in an elementary school, right? Clearly, not Hampton Hills Elementary. Then her dental crown popped off while flossing and fell down the sink. And then, to add the final icing on the cake, while she sat in her dentist's chair to have the crown replaced, her apartment building caught fire. So when Franny asked if she could come up for the weekend to help stock Merrily for the season, Kylie wondered if fate had toyed with her life once again.

"Franny? Can you help me with this box? I'm about to drop it and break every one of the—" She turned around and slammed to a halt, her eyes landing on her godmother, a warm smile on her wrinkled face, before sliding over to the man seated at the table beside her.

Suddenly the box fell from her grasp, slamming to the ground with a boom, followed by the distinct sound of glass shattering. A lot of glass.

"Fudge a monkey!" Kylie yelled.

Brady Littleton's eyebrows lifted, a smile tipping his lips, and instantly, Kylie wished she could go back outside and come in again. Maybe some magic would happen, and he wouldn't be there the second time around.

"What are you doing here?" Kylie asked, her breathing becoming shallow, her heart thumping in her chest. Tears burned her eyes at the mere sight of him, but Kylie refused to let them fall.

"Meeting with Ms. Franny. What are you doing here?" He leaned back in his chair, causing the front legs to rise off the ground, and crossed his arms. The crooked smile he wore around at eighteen flashed at her. It was the kind of smile that said nothing and no one could shake him, but there was a hint of something else in his eyes—something that looked an awful lot like fear. Kylie knew because she was feeling the same vomit-inducing fear that very moment.

"I asked you first."

His eyebrows lifted again, clear amusement on his face. "You did... and I answered you."

"No, you said that you were meeting with Franny. You didn't say why."

"You didn't ask why."

It took everything in her to keep from stomping her foot in aggravation. But she suspected that wouldn't paint her as a put-together adult, which she was...sort of. Instead, she gritted her teeth together and forced a smile. "Fine. Why are you talking to Franny?"

"What, do you own her now? I've gotta go through you to get permission to talk to her?"

Clearly, that annoying trait of his was still intact. "She's my godmother. And is it me, or are you refusing to be straight with me?" She shook her head and eyed the floor, then muttered under her breath, "I guess some people don't change."

His chair dropped to all fours with a clang, and he braced his hands against the table. "Want straight? Here it is, sweetheart: I'm here to buy Merrily Christmas so Franny can finally retire."

"What?" Kylie's hands shook at her sides, or maybe the whole room was shaking. It was hard to tell with this amount of anger erupting inside her. "Um, no you're not. I'm taking over this shop. Me. No one else. So you can take yourself right out of here." Kylie pointed to the door, then crossed her arms, her eyes locked on Brady. She ignored the pounding in her chest, the way it felt as though her heart had dropped a few inches. The ache was almost too much to take, but now she had a new emotion to tie to Brady Littleton—rage.

Slowly, he stood up, like he knew a fight was coming and wanted to show off that giant height of his. But he could forget intimidation—she wasn't backing down.

"Yeah, I don't think I'm leaving just because you asked me to," he said, his tone far too relaxed for the moment. Didn't he feel the temperature spike in the room? "See, I didn't schedule a meeting with you, now did I? I scheduled it with Franny." Brady cocked his head, and it was the first time Kylie noticed that his hair was buzzed short, very Channing Tatum or Bradley Cooper—very adult and different from the shaggy chin-length waves he had when they were teens. And yet…the look couldn't have been hotter on him.

Somehow that angered her all the more.

"Well, seeing as how Franny asked me to take over managing the shop, your meeting isn't with Franny. It's with me. I'll be sure to check my schedule to see when I can work you in, but I wouldn't get my hopes up. I'm very busy these days. It's the start of the holiday season, and, you might remember, that's our busiest time of the year." She snapped her fingers. "Oh, that's right. You decided to quit right before Christmas the last time I saw you. Probably don't remember how things are then. So let me tell you." She took a deliberate step forward, then two, until she stood in front of him. Her entire body shook now, but she wasn't sure if it was from her anger or the surge of emotions swirling around in her stomach. How could he still have this effect on her? "I don't care about anything you had scheduled before I got here. I'm here now. And this is my—I mean, Franny's shop. We're not selling."

Brady squinted his eyes and stared back at her, and the tension in the room rose to the ceiling, a thousand memories mixing with her anger and frustration until Kylie thought she might scream.

"Right. Well, I'll let you get to cleaning up that mess. I'd forgotten how clumsy you were." He nodded to the box of broken ornaments, and Kylie cursed under her breath for dropping it. She needed to come across as cool and collected and, okay, super sexy. But instead, her curls were a mess around her head, and she'd forgotten whether she put on makeup that morning. And then there was the hole in her leggings and the oversized T-shirt she'd thrown on because she couldn't find anything else clean.

Brady stepped around her and out the back door, which was supposed to be for staff only. He paused before leaving. "And just so we're clear: you will meet with me. I'll be here every day until you find the time. 'Cause I've got all the time in the world to close this deal."

Kylie chucked a stuffed reindeer at the door, but not before it closed, the aggravating man who'd once been her everything long gone.

"Yeah, we'll see about that."

Chapter 2

Brady made his way into Captain Jack's for dinner with his brothers. The restaurant sat along the shore of the Cherokee Lake, and like always, it smelled of fried fish, steaks, and beer. The evening crowd hadn't filtered in yet, so Brady took his time walking inside—partially because he wasn't in a hurry to be social, and partially because walking hurt.

His muscles were tight from his run and his hour-long weightlifting that afternoon. He'd intended to work off a little steam, all in an effort to get Kylie out of his mind, but after hours of pushing his body to the max, he discovered there was no denying the truth—his ex was back.

He thought of the look on her face when she first saw him, some combination of excitement and anger. It had been more than ten years since he'd last seen her, and yet she hadn't changed all that much. Her hair was still perfect chocolate waves, her eyes still deep brown, and he knew if he'd been closer to her he would have caught the flecks of gold swimming in the brown.

But whereas seventeen-year-old Kylie had been short and small-boned, adult Kylie now had curves in all the right places.

"You a little distracted?"

Brady's attention snapped to his right to find his two brothers seated by the windows. He'd almost walked right past them. "Guess so."

"Here, ordered you a cold one." Charlie slid a beer over to him, that pitying look of his flashing across his face before he could wipe it away. "Looks like you need one."

Normally, he'd put on his game face around his brothers, but after the run-in with Kylie, he didn't have the will to fake it. "I need a six-pack, and even that won't get it done." He ran his hands through his cropped hair, aggravated that he couldn't yank on the buzzed strands the way he could his long hair. Yet another thing Kylie had taken from him.

"So what happened with Franny?" Zac asked, taking a long pull of his own beer. "You get everything settled?"

Brady laughed sarcastically. "Hardly. I ran into a roadblock."

"Roadblock?" Charlie asked.

"She's back in town."

"She?" Charlie asked. "Ohhhh, *she*. Damn, really?"

"Yeah, apparently, she plans to take over the Christmas shop and keep the thing running so Franny can retire."

His brothers shared a look, and Brady knew what they were thinking without either having to say it. This was trouble on so many levels he couldn't decide what to focus on first. "I know what you're thinking."

"All right," Zac said. "Then how about you tell us what *you're* thinking. How are you after seeing her?"

Lost.

Sad.

So damn excited I almost kissed her.

"Fine." Brady shrugged. "What did you expect? A meltdown? It was a long time ago."

Charlie's eyebrows lifted and Brady chucked a chip from the basket of chips and salsa on the table at him. "Stop."

"I didn't say anything," Charlie said with raised hands.

"You were thinking it."

It was Zac who answered. "So, what? We're allowed to worry about you. How the hell can you possibly be fine? Kylie is back."

Brady blanched at the name, but he refused to show any other emotion. Anything at all would reveal the truth—he was one Kylie sighting away from losing his mind. "I'm fine, all right? Now, forget that crap. Let's talk about business. How are we going to convince Franny to sell us the shop now?"

The brothers exchanged another look and Brady sighed. "Fine, let's get this over with so I don't have to deal with calls later."

"All right, I'll play," Zac said. "You're all alone and the only girl you ever gave a damn about is back in town. Don't you think that's a sign or something?"

"So now you believe in signs? What has that wife of yours done to you?"

Zac's wife Sophie was one of those insanely natural, organic types, so it wouldn't surprise him a bit if she were into destiny and that crap, too.

"Beside the point."

"Says who?" Brady pushed, eager to change the subject to anything but him. "You going all loony is all kinds of on point. We need you helping run this business, especially with the expansion. Which *is going* to happen, even if she thinks she can walk back into town and take over everything that's mine all over again."

Zac leaned back in his chair. "Right. She's no big deal."

With a long sigh, Brady ran his hands over his cropped hair, then got aggravated at the reminder of why he cut it and dropped his hands to the table. "Where's Lee? I need another." He pointed to the beer, then glanced around, eager to look at anything but one of his brothers. He felt their concerning stares without him needing to look over at them to confirm it.

"Maybe go over and talk to her. Just air it all out and then y'all can talk about the shop," Charlie offered. He was always the problem solver of the family, but the thing with Kylie wasn't something that could be talked out. What happened, the things that were said…you couldn't undo those things, couldn't unsay those things.

Some disasters couldn't be repaired.

Still, before all that, before the actions and words and hurt, they'd been something else. Brady and Kylie were the couple everyone else watched, the ones people smiled at and said they wanted their own Brady or Kylie. They were perfect and so in love the word itself sounded stupid, because what they had was so much more.

Now it seemed even stupider to think that what they had was real. How could you find your soul mate at seventeen? That kind of love wasn't real, everyone knew it, and yet…

"Y'all need anything?" Lee asked as he came over to take away their empty dinner plates.

Charlie eyed him. "You having another?"

But suddenly Brady no longer wanted another drink. He wanted to be alone with his thoughts.

"Nah, I'll probably head on out. Gotta come up with a new game plan for Franny."

Lee dropped their check, and Brady reached for it first, forever eager to prove to his brothers that he cared about the family. He screwed that up once, and he never intended to do it again.

"You paid last time," Zac said. "I got this one."

"It's good. You got a family to finance. I'm just me." And though the words were true, they were hard to digest. He was alone. Financially secure, sure. Free to do whatever the hell he wanted, yes. But alone, all the same.

Zac stared at him again, seeing through the simple words to the thoughts underneath, just as he had when they were kids and Brady had once again failed a test or shown up late to a ball game, only to be forced to sit in the dugout. He'd screwed up everything he touched for so many years that his brothers assumed he would disappointment them, so when he finally crawled out of his selfish ass and started being a decent person, it took them years to actually believe him.

Then his dad's heart attack happened, and Brady's character was questioned once again. He spent years rebuilding that trust, but the need to prove to them that he wouldn't let them down, that he wouldn't fail the family, still lingered below his confidence.

The restaurant was filling up now, and Brady needed to disappear into himself. He'd always been the kind of person that could only handle a crowd for so long. Like a pretend extrovert, he could do the social thing, but deep down it was hard for him, and he needed a break to get his thoughts back to neutral.

"Keep the change," Brady said, passing the check back to Lee. He downed the last of his beer, then clasped hands with Charlie and patted Zac's back. "See y'all tomorrow."

To their credit, they let Brady leave without more aggravation, and he got into his red Z06, parked at the road because hell if he would drive down Captain Jack's gravel road. He started down the road, unsure when he'd decided to drive past Franny's house, but he found himself turning right instead of left and then following the long stretch of road toward Franny's. He didn't know what he thought he'd find there, and that unknown scared him enough that he almost turned around. But Brady had always been a curious person. He wondered if he'd see another car in the driveway—a car that was sure to be Kylie's. He had no right to seek her out, and shouldn't after how things ended. She could be with someone else now, could have someone in town with her. Even a family. But something told him it was just her, which meant what? That she'd struggled to move on, too? That she thought about him as often as he thought about her?

Slowing the car, he crept past the house, only to find it dark except for a single light shining out from the second story. He knew without question that Kylie would be in that room, likely working late into the night to find a way to save Franny's. Because that was who she was—the heart she had—and even though they'd fallen apart, he still considered her to be the kindest, best person he'd ever known.

He stopped the car on the road and peered up at the light again. There was no one on the road, only him, so if she looked out the window and saw his headlights, she would know that he was there, and she would know that he was there for her.

"How am I supposed to forget you now?" he asked. Then the sheer curtains in the window swayed and a form appeared. She was in pajamas, her hair a mess on the top of her head, glasses over her eyes because she'd long since taken out her contacts. It'd been forever since he'd seen her, and yet it felt as though no time had passed at all.

He could just as easily be in his old Mustang. Just as easily sneak up the trellis and into her room at Franny's, where she would stay more often than at her own house. And never once did her parents notice or care.

Before the moment drew long and before she could walk away from him again, he put the car in drive and pulled away, his chest tight, the weight that had slowly lifted over the years now clamped back in place.

He needed to figure out how to get this woman out of his head and heart before she destroyed him for good.

* * * *

Kylie dropped the curtain and took a step back, her skin clammy despite the chill in the old house. Surely that wasn't...it couldn't have been. And yet she knew with every ounce of her being that it was Brady. The question was why.

Her thoughts went back to the last time he'd been outside Franny's house, pellets of rain beating down all around him, a look of resolution on his face.

He had stared at her, and she stared back and wordlessly opened her window. It took longer than normal for him to crawl up the trellis, or maybe it was the anticipation of him getting there that made it feel longer.

But then he was there, in her room, his hair slick against his forehead and his clothes dripping on the hardwood, and without a thought she reached out, the decision made before she'd consciously decided to make it, and her hands went to his shirt. Easing it off, she dropped it to the floor, and then he undid his shorts and they fell to the floor with a clang that should have worried them, but the moment held them in place.

Brady was slow, gentle in the best and worst possible ways. She wanted to feel him all around her, on her, in her.

They were seventeen and so full of hope for their lives that it seemed impossible that the most important night for them would end up being the beginning of the end.

Shaking off the memory, Kylie sat down on her bed. A sinking feeling worked through her at the thought of their last year together, each month more painful than the last, until she landed on the last time she saw him and she couldn't stay in the thought anymore.

Grabbing her robe, she draped it around her shoulders, even though she wasn't cold, and shoved each of her feet into her bedroom shoes. She stepped out of her room and rounded the banister, the old wooden steps creaking as she walked, and then she padded down the hall and into the kitchen. Sure enough, Franny sat at the table in the breakfast nook, crocheting like always.

"Can't sleep?" she asked without looking up. Franny had always been a night owl who pretended to go to bed early, which likely meant she knew when Brady was here all those years ago, even if she pretended not to notice.

"You know I'll be up until one."

Franny nodded. "So much like your mom."

Kylie wanted to ask Franny not to say that, but she knew that Franny was far too nice to ever see her friend as the selfish woman she was. "I guess."

"Can I make you some tea?" she asked without looking up.

"I'll make it."

The wind picked up outside, a cold front blowing in that would give the kids in town a thrill as meteorologists talked about the potential for snow. Immediately, Kylie thought of kids' crafts to do at the shop—ornaments, snowmen, mini globes. She made a note to check Pinterest later so she could pull a supply list together.

"You seem deep in thought today," Franny said, once again not looking up, but this time Kylie knew it was less to do with her focus on her project and more on respecting Kylie's need to reflect on questions like that without being watched.

Kylie put the kettle on the stovetop and clicked on the gas stove eye. "Can you tell me something?"

"Of course."

"Are you tired of the shop? Is that why you want to sell?"

Franny's hands paused for the first time. "I don't want to sell. I would never dream of selling my shop. You might remember, it was my mother's, and I inherited it from her."

"You used to say she worked even when she was asleep at night."

A smile spread across Franny's face. "She had a lot of great ideas and would wake to jot them down. She made the shop what it is, so when I took over, I wanted to continue that legacy."

"So then why sell to Brady? Why even talk to him? Why not go to the bank?"

The kettle whistled from behind her, so Kylie gave Franny a moment to think while she turned off the eye and moved the kettle to a cooler one. Taking two teacups from the cabinet beside the refrigerator, she filled each with hot water, then dropped a teabag into each to steep. She walked over, set one before Franny, and took the seat across from her.

"I know you don't like to worry me, but let me help you."

Franny stared down at her teacup, then slowly glanced up at Kylie, tears in her eyes now. "You're right, I don't like to worry you. But you deserve to know the truth. I can't afford to keep the shop open, and I am too old to consider a loan from the bank. I wouldn't live long enough to pay it off."

"Don't say—"

She lifted a hand to stop Kylie. "Some things are just true, dear. Saying them out loud or ignoring them doesn't change the facts. If my family history is any indication, my days are numbered. Without a loan, it would take a miracle to keep the shop running."

Yeah, but that didn't mean Kylie had to let this happen. She knew Franny as well as she knew herself, and it would break her heart to lose the shop. The thought made Kylie's heart ache in a way it hadn't in years. Franny was the only one she had left, the only person to ever truly care about her. Of course, she'd once thought that tiny group of people who cared about her was two, but Brady had shown her that he only cared about himself.

And then, as though a light bulb had popped on inside her mind, an idea occurred to her.

She sat up abruptly, her thoughts spinning. Brady cared about himself more than anyone else, so what if Kylie presented him with an offer that benefited him, an offer he couldn't refuse?

Grabbing her keys and her purse, Kylie started for the door, too excited to remember that she'd just made tea for her and Franny.

"Where are you going?" Franny called.

Kylie grinned over her shoulder at her godmother. "To find our miracle."

Chapter 3

Brady sighed heavily as he leaned back in his office chair. The walls of his office were a muted gray with off white trim. His desk was antiqued oak, and his chair was dark leather. Windows stretched from floor to ceiling on one wall, his finance degree from USC on the adjacent wall, and then shelves lined the back wall. A variety of books sat on the shelving, many he hadn't touched, but some of his favorites showed wear from him reading them again and again.

These days his reading interests veered on the nonfiction side, almost always around business as he tried to keep up-to-date on trends and strategies.

But tonight he hadn't time to think about reading. He'd been poring over the numbers Zac had provided him for the expansion for over an hour, all in an effort to figure out how to persuade Ms. Franny into selling. But at the end of the day, their goals for the space didn't hold the same emotional tie that she would have to the Christmas shop. Which, in truth, was the reason he'd taken so long to pursue her. How could he go to her and ask her to sell her shop knowing how much it meant to her (and, at one point, to him)?

He thought of the time he and Kylie had gotten stranded there, a winter storm blowing in so fiercely that the roads weren't safe to drive on. They were smart enough to not take the chance. They ended up baking cookies in the mini cookie oven Franny bought that year and watching Christmas movie after Christmas movie. Finally, just after midnight, the power went out and they bundled together under some of the down blankets Franny sold in the shop. They talked about everything and nothing as snow fell outside, until they were too tired to keep their eyes open.

Still to this day, it was the best night of his life, the night whatever was happening between them became more.

Finishing off a water bottle, Brady tossed it into the trash and stared at his laptop again. Still, he couldn't think up a sales pitch that would work on Franny. He needed a break. And a beer.

Brady pushed his chair back and stood up, stretched until the joints in his back popped, then started out into the hall toward the kitchen. The kitchen, like the rest of the house, was five sizes larger than what he needed, complete with a double oven and two dishwashers, more cabinet space than he'd ever fill, and a large eat-in area that would seat eight.

The house itself had four bedrooms and three and a half baths, but the original owners had been builders so they went all out with the details. Everything about it was custom, down to the shade of the hardwood floors, which had been a custom blend for the builder's wife. Then life stepped in, and she passed away from ovarian cancer. The builder said he couldn't live in the house he'd built for her any longer.

Brady paid the builder's asking price, even though he could have offered less and the builder would have likely taken it. He had never been the kind of man to kick another when he was down, so he finalized everything with the bank, paid what he had to pay out of pocket, and moved on in.

For weeks, he'd gone from room to room, trying to find ways to make the house his own, paint, decor, whatever. But every time he attempted to move something, he felt a punch of guilt, like the wife was there watching him move her stuff. He ended up leaving it exactly as it was, with the exception of buying a few pieces of furniture, gutting the master bedroom, remodeling the office. The rest didn't matter to him anyway.

Light rain pinged against the tin roof, and Brady made a note to check the weather for the next few days to see if they'd get any snow. It was early for snow, but then last year, Crestler's Key had its first snow in late November.

He opened his fancy fridge and pulled out a beer, his third of the day, and felt a tinge of disappointment in himself. He tried to limit drinking, but these weren't normal times. Kylie was back, and with her return, all the memories he'd tucked away came pouring back. Suddenly, he didn't know how to go about his day in the same way, how to be in this town, without his thoughts conjuring up all the what-ifs that he'd tried to ignore over the years.

Cracking the can, he took a drink, then went to the pantry and pulled out some pretzels. He'd just decided to call it quits on the business stuff in favor of finding something good on TV when a knock at the front door pulled his attention from the bag of pretzels and to the random visitor.

No one came to see him except his family, and they would all be busy with their own families at this hour.

Another knock, and Brady set down his beer, but kept still. He was one of those people who despite all the lights being on and the TV playing would freeze up and pretend not to be there in hopes that a random visitor would go away.

But another knock, then three more came, and Brady knew whoever it was wouldn't go away any time soon.

Brady padded around the kitchen island, cognizant of the fact that he wore nothing but an A-shirt and his usual red plaid pajama pants, his feet bare. He peeked out the side window, and immediately his chest tightened, the desire to flee so real it took all his effort to remain rooted to the spot.

Taking his time, he turned the deadbolt, then the lock on the handle, and eased the door open, his body blocking the rest of his house from view like he needed to protect it—or himself—from the person standing before him.

"What are you doing here?"

"I need to talk to you. Can I come in?"

Brady stared down at Kylie, the person who'd once been so much a part of his world she didn't bother to knock when she came over. And yet now, here she stood, asking if she could come in. Even more surprising, he was tempted to say no.

She wore simple black leggings and a long pullover, Uggs on her feet, the look so very Kylie-like that it made his heart clench. She had always been the kind of woman that preferred to dress in clothes as comfortable as PJs, and it'd always been something he loved about her.

"Is that a yes or no, or were you going to just continue to stare at me?"

His eyes narrowed as her hands went to her curvy hips. She was shaking, whether from anger or nerves he couldn't be sure. "I'm thinking about it."

"All right, let me help you with that." She pushed past him and into his house, and Brady contemplated grabbing her little ass and taking her back outside. This was his house, his world, and she made it very apparent years ago that she wanted no part of it.

"Hey, I didn't invite you in." Brady knew it was a moot point, but he needed to maintain some semblance of control. Though he'd never once had control when Kylie was around. That was part of the problem.

"I didn't ask you to invite me in." She paused in the foyer, her eyes darting right then left, then straight ahead, taking it all in.

Like the rest of the house, the foyer was custom in every way. Decorative marble flooring, wood and stone columns leading into the formal dining room, a chandelier so nice it had no business being in Brady's house, yet there it hung above them.

"Wow, I didn't expect you to be…" She ducked her head into the dining room, took in the large table, the mismatched chairs that somehow went together perfectly. Shelves lined the wall across from them, where there had once been fine china on display. Brady had forced the builder to take it with him when he left. Ornate curtains framed the double windows, with a second set of sheer curtains tucked inside the larger ones. It all made no sense to Brady, but he had learned over the year and half that he'd lived in the builder's house that his wife had a design aesthetic that was all her own.

If Brady had a wife, he might have liked her to make the house her own, but then the closest he'd come to even entertaining such a word walked out of his life, only to crash back into it like a freaking meteor.

"Didn't expect me to be what?"

Kylie adjusted her pullover in the front and then the back, an anxious tic no doubt, and he settled on that she wasn't so much angry as nervous. He knew the feeling.

She rotated around to face him. "I didn't expect you to be married." Her eyes diverted the moment she said the word, and he had to wonder if it was as hard for her to entertain him being with someone else as it was for him to think of her with someone.

He crossed his arms and leaned against one of the columns. "Who said I was married?"

Kylie gestured around them. "Someone had to decorate this house."

Brady stared at her. "Someone did."

He knew he should say more, squash her fears and all, but he couldn't bring himself to give her the relief she so clearly craved, when her being there made him want to vomit.

Her eyes widened a touch before she corrected. "Right. Well, if I'm disturbing you, then I can—"

"Ky, what are you doing here?"

Pausing mid-motion, she faced him again, and this time he caught the sadness in her eyes. He almost asked her what was wrong, but it wasn't his right to ask that question, and he'd long ago told himself that he didn't care.

"I'm waiting."

"I'm answering."

"Doesn't sound like it."

Kylie huffed and planted her hands on her hips again. "Are you going to let me talk or are we going to go around again?"

The truth was Brady didn't want her to talk. He wanted her out of his house so he could feel like himself again. "All right, I'm listening."

She drew a long breath and peered over her shoulder, then back, then over her shoulder again in a double-take. "Wow, is that your kitchen?" And then before he could ask her what she was doing or answer the question, she took off again, farther into his house and into his world. Each step felt like she was making a permanent impression there, like the house could relax now, knowing a female hand had returned. He wanted no part of any of it.

"Where are you going now?"

"To check out this fancy kitchen." She ran a hand over the granite countertops. "God, this must have cost you a fortune."

The truth was it had cost him far more than he should have paid, and yet far less than the house was worth. But at the time, Zac and Charlie were setting up house and looking all responsible and adult-like, and he was what? Living in the same old apartment, partying with the same women, hitting up the same spots on Friday night. It all became too much. So he shut off that life and decided to settle down. Even if he had no one to settle down with, he could at least buy a nice house.

"It was enough."

She grinned, and it was so like her that Brady forgot what he was going to say next. "Sounds like something you would say. Well, whoever she is, she has good taste."

"She does." Once again their eyes met, and he couldn't keep up the charade any longer. "The original owner was a builder. He built the house with his wife, every inch of it custom built and made for her. And then she died. He couldn't bring himself to live here without her, so I bought it to save him the trouble."

For a moment, Kylie stared at him, her expression unreadable.

"What?" Brady asked.

"Nothing," she said, looking away. But it was clear she was having thoughts about this, and once again, Brady wished she hadn't come. He couldn't think, couldn't settle down. She had him on edge in his own house. He needed her to leave.

"Why are you here, Kylie?" he asked, unable to hide the exhaustion in his voice. Being around her made it so hard to pretend that everything was okay. "I'm guessing it's not to check out my kitchen."

"No…it's not. I came here to offer you a compromise." She swallowed, then eyed the Keurig on the counter. "Since when do you drink coffee?"

"Since I started getting less than five hours of sleep a night. You were saying something about a compromise?"

The rain had picked up outside, creating a peaceful melody. There was once a time when Brady would have considered it romantic, nothing but Kylie and him and the sound of rain. But those days had come and gone.

"I came up with an idea that I think could work for both of us."

"I'm listening."

"So Franny can't afford to keep the shop running as is. You know that and I know that, and she's refusing to try to secure a loan that could tide her over. At the same time, she doesn't want to sell, and I'm willing to do whatever I can to help her keep her shop."

Brady went over to the Keurig and pushed the button to turn it on, then pivoted back around and crossed his arms again. At Kylie's raised eyebrows he said, "Thought we may need coffee for this. Unless you stopped drinking it."

"I'd rather stop breathing air."

A small smile cracked on his face before he could stop it, and Kylie offered her own in return. It was warm and honest, so unlike most of the women Brady knew. He bet Kylie didn't own lipstick *or* lip gloss. God, he was in trouble.

"Go on."

"Franny said you were wanting to buy the shop so you would have additional space for Southern Dive. So what if we agreed to split Franny's? Of course, you would pay for half the shop now."

And now Brady's smile was full out glowing. "You're joking, right? What sense would it make for me to pay you for half of a dying business?"

Kylie stared him down, her eyes fixed on his. "First off, it's the building you want, not the business, so don't talk to me like I'm clueless about this whole thing. I'm not. And second, Merrily Christmas isn't just any business, and I would be willing to bet that it bothers you to take it from Franny. Forget all that happened between us. You cared about Franny. Likely still do. And you never hurt those you care about."

He almost said *unlike you* but managed to stop himself.

"What do you say? Will you let us keep half of the shop?"

Brady thought about the offer, what it would mean for him and his brothers. They would still have the space they needed for shipments, and even better, they could test out how much space they needed with less risk and investment. But there was no way he could allow Kylie to come to his house and get him to just accept what she was offering. Not after the way things ended with them.

"Until Christmas."

A confused look crossed her face. "What's until Christmas?"

"I'll buy half the business to give Franny—and you—an opportunity to increase business. But if you can't, if the business is still in the red come December 25, then you agree to let me buy the remainder of the space at half what I pay now."

"What? Are you crazy? I'm not interested in giving away Franny's building."

"And I'm not interested in charity." Guilt punched him in the stomach the moment the word slipped from his lips, but he couldn't bring himself to show it. Not now. Not with Kylie here, messing up his life. "We will buy half now and the remainder at a fifty percent discount. Set a sales goal to include in the contract. I'll even give you to the end of the year. If you succeed, then you get to maintain half the space. If not, it's ours at fifty percent off. Take it or leave it."

Her teeth ground together, fire in her eyes, as she stepped up to him. Brady thought she might deck him, but instead, she held out her hand. "Fine. It's a deal."

He slid his hand into hers and closed, and it was as though time stopped. No, like time rewound and they were teens again, his body numb, his heart full for the first time in forever. A tingly feeling spread from their hands, to his wrist, almost to his forearm, before he found the will to pull away.

"I'll have the papers drawn up and to you tomorrow," he said, avoiding eye contact.

Kylie nodded. "You do that." Then she reached around Brady for one of the coffee cups he'd pulled from his cabinet, placed the cup in the correct spot of the Keurig, and hit the large size. He wasn't sure what bothered him more—that she was making herself coffee in his house or that she knew he'd have a k-cup ready in the dispenser.

The coffee finished brewing, tension igniting between them with each passing second. She pulled the mug away and drew in the aroma, a slow smile curling her lips. "I love the smell of coffee, don't you?"

"Want access to my fridge, too? Or better yet, why don't you make yourself at home in my bed." She flinched, and Brady grinned.

"Nah, I take mine black now." Then she started toward the door, an obvious sway to her step.

"You're welcome, by the way. And I expect you to return that cup," he called, only to hear the click of his door closing in answer. And just like that, she'd gotten under his skin. Again.

Chapter 4

Kylie unlocked the back door of Merrily Christmas, humming the Christmas song she'd been listening to in her car.

Franny had spent the last week training her on all the changes she'd implemented at the shop since Kylie had left. When Kylie worked there as a teen, purchases were made with cash and jotted down in a spiral-bound order book. Now, Franny used some point-of-sale software that was linked to the credit card machine, the cash register, and maintained an inventory count. Adding new inventory was still a pain—double checking it against the packing slip, adding a marked up cost to it, then tagging it—but it was worth the effort on the back end.

She pushed the door open with her back side, then edged inside, the cookie oven in one arm, a Keurig in the other, the two boxes sandwiched together, else one or the both would be on the ground by now.

Her humming and good mood turned into song. "Jingle all the way, oh what fun it is to ride in a one horse open—what the hell do you think you're doing?"

Brady turned slowly, a crooked grin on his face at the sight of her. He held one of her ornament boxes in his hands. "You never could carry a tune."

Her eyes narrowed. "And you never could answer a direct question. I asked you what you were doing."

"Did you bring in my coffee cup this time or do I need to come to Franny's to get it back?"

"Again, avoiding the question." The truth was Kylie loved that mug, and fully intended to keep it for the rest of her life. "And who are they?" she asked, pointing to two men carrying in a long, rectangular table.

Brady called over to them. "Hold it. I need to move a few more of these boxes." He dropped the box he'd been holding onto the floor and pushed it with his foot out of the way. Forget the fact that DELICATE was written all over the dang thing.

Kylie's jaw clenched tight. "I ask again, what in the hell do you think you're doing?"

Brady pressed a finger to his lips. "*Shh*, we have kids in the room," he said, gesturing to the men, who Kylie now realized were teenagers. Though what kind of teenagers didn't go to school on a Monday? Clearly, the kind who associated with Brady.

"Answer the question."

He sighed. "If you must know, I'm moving in my packaging table."

"And who exactly approved you to do that? We agreed to split half the shop, not have you take whatever you want and move whatever you want. This is still my—I mean, Franny's—shop."

They glared at one another. Tension radiated between them, sparking and rolling, until Kylie worried about Brady's well-being, because she was seconds away from taking his head off.

"Actually, Franny did. And as you mentioned, it's her shop, not yours. She said I could take this side of the stockroom. So here I am. Do you have a problem with that?"

Yes. Yes, she had a major problem with it. With all of this. But what could she say?

"From now on, you need to pass any requests by me before doing them. I handle our inventory and the stockroom. If I can't find something, it presents a problem when I'm restocking things."

Brady cocked his head, thought for a moment, then shook it in disagreement. "Nah, I don't think so. I'm not a tenant of yours. I'm half owner of this building, or did you not receive the paperwork?"

She rolled back on her heels at the blow. Of course she had received the paperwork, and she read every single page word for word. Somehow she'd hoped to find the words JUST KIDDING at the end and this whole thing would be a dream. The idea of working day in and day out with the man who'd single-handedly shattered her heart years ago was enough to make her contemplate setting up an appointment with Dr. Shattles, Crestler's Key's one and only therapist.

With new resolve, she drew a breath and set down the cookie oven and Keurig, then drew another breath and pivoted slowly. She marched over to Brady and lifted her chin. "Listen and listen good. I make the rules here, not you. I have a system in here. I'm happy to share the space with you, but I have to move things in an organized manner first. Either that works for you or it doesn't. I haven't signed those papers you gave me yet, and neither has Franny, so if this doesn't work for you, then I am happy to tear them up and figure things out on my own. Wouldn't be the first time," she added under her breath, and Brady swallowed hard.

He opened his mouth to reply when Franny walked in from the front of the shop, a stern look on her face directed at both of them. "Now listen, you two, this can be easy or it can be hard, and since my name is still the only name on this building, neither of yours, we're going to do things my way. The easy way. Brady—you get the right half of the stockroom and the right half of the store. Do what you please there, but we would appreciate it if you gave us an opportunity to move our own things. Somehow I doubt you'll use the same care we would." Her eyes fell to the stack of boxes beside him, each box stacked haphazardly. It looked like a gust of wind could knock the whole stack over.

"Right. No problem, Ms. Franny. Anything you ask."

Kylie tsked. "Anything *she* asks, so me asking isn't enough for you, right?"

"And you," Franny said, cutting her off and pointing at her goddaughter. "None of this over-the-top, OCD mess. Move things and organize as best you can, but our space was just cut in half. You'll have to improvise, which I'm sure you can do. And if you need an extra set of muscles when moving things around, I'm sure Brady here is happy to help."

"Happy to offer my muscles to you any time you need them," he said with a grin.

Kylie crossed her arms and shot daggers at her ex. "Yeah, I don't think so. I don't need your help."

"Typical," Brady murmured under his breath.

Franny grinned over at them, said something like "Some things never change," then disappeared back into the front of the shop. The two teenagers were still holding the table, and Kylie felt like a jerk. "Put that down wherever. I'll get the rest out of the way." She brushed the dust from her hands onto her jeans and then went over, careful to avoid Brady's stare, grabbed a box, and edged back around the table. She made her way over to her own long rectangular table, hers a place to make wreaths and other decor that customers could buy. She set down the box, then turned to go for another, only to find Brady picking up two and following after her. Their eyes locked, and a flurry erupted in her stomach before she could suppress it.

"You don't have to do that."

He set the boxes down beside her first box and then stared down at her. They were two feet apart, yet it felt like mere inches separated them. He was too close. Far too close.

"I know I don't have to. I want to."

Their eyes met again, then one of the teens called to Brady and he cleared his throat before turning away to see what he needed. Kylie took the opportunity to draw a long, much-needed breath.

What was that? Certainly not feelings. There could be, would be, no feelings here. What she needed was to focus...and stay far, far away from her ex until her heart remembered that she was over him. Way, way, way over him.

She peeked over her shoulder, took in the way his T-shirt stretched across the contours of his back, the way his jeans hugged his—

Brady spun around at that moment, and Kylie jerked back, her hand colliding with the box she'd just set on the table and narrowly knocking it onto the floor had she not grabbed it.

"You all right?" he called out.

"Who me?" Kylie fumbled with the box, her hands shaking now. Then she grinned over at him, before trying to steady the box and in turn almost pushing another off the table. Because clearly she'd forgotten how to function. "Yep, perfect. Just need to..." She pointed to the door to the front of the store, and then disappeared through it before he could ask anything else. Or she could do anything else to let on just how rattled she felt.

"You all right?" Franny asked.

"Yes, why do people keep asking me that?"

Franny's eyebrows lifted. "Maybe because you're speaking in shrill."

"I am not."

"You are. Ally will tell you."

"Who?"

Franny pointed to the register, where a young woman stood staring between them like she wasn't sure whether she should speak or keep quiet.

"Tell her, Ally."

Ally's face shifted from surprise to fear before finally she released a breath and shook her head. "Girl, I could hear you from outside before I came in." Then the fear returned. "Please don't fire me."

Franny laughed. "Kylie meet Ally, our new part-time help for the holiday season. Ally meet Kylie, my goddaughter, who has officially named herself shop manager. I'm going down to AJ&P for some breakfast. I'll let you two get acquainted."

Franny grinned like she'd just made the biggest joke in the world, and Kylie got the feeling that despite what Kylie felt was a reality, Franny would always be the true manager of Merrily Christmas.

"Hi, sorry about that," she said to the new hire. "I swear I'm not crazy or anything."

"Debatable."

Gritting her teeth, she peered over her shoulder to find Brady smiling at her from the other side of the room. She hadn't heard him come out from the back, which meant he had heard the entire exchange with Franny. Fantastic.

"No one was talking to you." She focused back on Ally, prepared to do a formal introduction, when Brady's laughter cut through again.

Kylie closed her eyes. "Deep breath. Deep, long breath." She opened her eyes to find Ally smiling sympathetically at her. "Franny told you."

"A bit," she said with a shrug. "I can't imagine it's easy."

The store was open now and a few shoppers had come in, which meant Kylie would need to watch the shrillness. "No, but enough about my drama. Is this your first time working here or have you worked the season before?"

Ally laughed. "Nah, I'm well versed in the crazy here. I try to help every holiday season as I can. I'm a mom of a precious five-year-old, so I can only work part time. But honestly, I love it. I love the way people light up when they come in here. It reminds me that there's a point to the season, ya know? Not just all the insanity. I think people want to go somewhere that feels magical. Give them magic, and they'll come again and again."

Kylie thought back to her childhood, to all the small things Franny would do to make the shop special, and an idea occurred to her—what if she created events at the shop? Daily craft days or specials or—"Oh my God. Why didn't I think of this before? You are a genius!"

"That's one name for me, but sure, I'll take it," Brady called.

She rolled her eyes. "Again, not talking to you."

Ally laughed again. "Girl, you're in trouble with that one."

"Don't I know it. But anyway, ignore him. I try to."

"How's that working out for you?"

Kylie's shoulders slumped. "Splendidly, as you can tell. Anyway, you gave me a great idea. So if people want a bit of magic, then maybe to help the shop get back to the level we need, we should give them a bit of holiday cheer. "

"Give them magic?"

"Yeah, in the form of holiday cheer and fun." Kylie realized the customers that had come in before had stopped to listen to her. "So maybe we have daily events—holiday craft days, holiday shopping fun, Santa day! The kids can come see Santa. We can even do a special little photo that they can take home with them. And coffee and cookies and tea every day. Give people a place to come that feels separate from all the rigors of their life and all the commercialism of the season that drives you crazy. What do you think?" She eyed Ally, then the customers, before her gaze caught on Brady, who had stopped working to listen. "I just...maybe if I can make it like it used to be, then Franny can keep her shop. Maybe I can save it."

Brady swallowed hard, then looked away, and Kylie forced herself to focus back on Ally, her thoughts on remedying more than just the shop.

"I love it," Ally said.

"Us, too," the older women said, excitedly. "You can count us as regulars."

Kylie smiled and the women went back to shopping.

Merrily was separated into villages, holiday decor, and then gift ideas. Franny had handmade candles brought in a few months ago, and they were very popular. The shop wasn't huge, but there was a lot to see. "Okay, maybe we should create a schedule," she said to Ally at the same time that Ally's phone chirped.

"Was that a bird ringtone?"

Ally's eyes went wide as she pulled her phone toward her face, typed away, then sighed loudly in aggravation. "Damn, already gone."

"What?"

She shook her head. "I'm trying to score a Real N Feel doll for my daughter for Christmas."

"Real N Feel?"

"You haven't heard of these things? It's like this robotic doll. They have boy and girl options, so little boys can get them, too. They're the hottest toy this season and the stupid manufacturer didn't anticipate the hype, so there aren't enough of them. A few websites have gone up that will track when stores get them in stock and send you an alert to your phone. That was the chirping you heard, but the dang doll gets snatched up before I can get there."

Kylie walked around to stand beside Ally and peered down at the phone. Sure enough, a site showed every retailer imaginable—Walmart, Toys "R" Us, Target, etc.—all of them with SOLD OUT beside the store name. Then at the bottom of the screen, there was a list of the most recent available inventory, all showing available for less than a minute before someone else grabbed it.

"Are they not available in store, too? Is it only online?"

"Oh, they're in store all right," Ally said, again exasperated. "But there are lines around the store before they open, all for people to try to get one of, like, three that the store gets. And Walmart gets their inventory so randomly that it's impossible to know when they will get theirs. My husband works long hours and leaves early in the morning. He's with the electric company. So I can't go wait at a Target two towns over for two or three hours, which is what it takes to get there early enough to grab one. And even then, you may not be lucky enough, because the store could have only gotten one. There's no way to know."

"That's horrible."

"It's so frustrating, and of course, this doll is the only thing Rena wants from Santa. I've been tempted to go on eBay, because there are all these horrible people buying them for retail and then marking them way up."

"Ugh, no."

"Yes. And I can't pay those prices."

More customers came in, and Ally pushed away from the counter. "So now you know my drama. Not as fun as yours, I'll admit," she said with a grin as she eyed Brady.

Kylie watched her go to greet the customers and decided that she would need to help Ally get this present.

She turned to find Brady setting up shelving along one of the walls on his side. He lifted his arms to put something on the top shelf, causing his T-shirt to lift and expose a sliver of plaid boxers.

Forget fun. Kylie's drama was downright painful.

Chapter 5

Brady pulled open the door to AJ&P bakery and held it for two older ladies to walk out. They smiled at him, and then went on their way, and Brady told himself that he was still a nice guy. That part hadn't changed after Kylie left. He just became more…guarded.

Or maybe he was just—

He shook his head to stop himself. Ever since Kylie came back to town, he couldn't stop thinking about all the things that had changed since she left. Namely with him. And in his search, it occurred to him that not a whole heck of a lot had. He wasn't sure if that was a good thing or a bad thing.

Needing to put it out of his mind, he stepped into the bakery/sandwich shop, the scent of fresh breads hitting him full on. Most people came to the shop to get a bowl of soup and a hot sandwich and ended up buying a plethora of baked goods instead. Especially his mother, which was why he'd asked to meet there for lunch.

"You're late," she said as he neared, then kissed her cheek.

"You sound surprised," he said with a grin.

Grace Littleton smiled back at her son. "Not surprised so much as forever hopeful that you'll buy a watch and make a point to look at it once in a while."

Brady took a sip from the ice water she'd already ordered for him, because he wasn't the only one who never changed. Likely the woman had already ordered food for the both of them and a to-go order of turnovers.

Sure enough, a minute later, the waitress brought over a plate for each of them: broccoli cheddar soup for his mom, hot ham and cheese for him.

He took a bite and groaned. "Either that's the best sandwich I've ever had or I'm starving."

His mother shot him a worried look. "You barely eat dinner, you can't also skip breakfast."

"I do breakfast," he said around another bite that was less a bite and more inhaling the whole thing. He eyed the front, curious if he could get the waitress's attention to order a second to go.

"Coffee doesn't count as breakfast. I'm worried about you. Your brothers said you've been working all hours of the day getting the shop's extension worked out." She kept her focus on him, waiting for his reaction, and he prayed he didn't give one.

It'd been a week since he'd moved things into the Christmas shop, and though a part of him spent time there because it was his job to make sure everything went perfectly, it was also because he didn't feel whole unless he was there. Like a part of him was missing and once he walked into that building, the void went away. He could push aside questions from his brothers about it, but his mother wouldn't be so easy to convince.

"I'm fine, Mom. I eat, I sleep, I work. Rinse, repeat. It's been that way for a long time now. Not sure it's going to change any time s…"

Brady trailed off as he caught the person passing by the bakery's window, and then the door opening, and her walking in, and suddenly all the air in his lungs swept out.

"Shit." He jerked back and looked over at his mom, because while he was a twenty-nine-year-old man, he still tried for decent language around her.

But instead of lecturing him, she stared at Kylie and said, "I'll say," then patted his hand, which was now gripping the edge of the table.

"I hadn't seen her yet. She looks…"

He focused back on the sandwich before him, but suddenly he was no longer hungry. "I know."

"And you're around her every day."

"Most."

His mother tapped his hand again, and he looked up. "If it makes you feel any better, it's probably hard for her, too."

"It's not hard. It's fine. I'm fine."

"Right."

Her eyes cut back to the register, and then a slow smile curled her lips, and he knew before she spoke that Kylie had spotted her.

"Mrs. Littleton, how are you?"

Brady sighed and turned to face the woman who'd single-handedly shattered his heart years ago and was now back in town to complete the job.

She stopped a few feet away from them. "Brady…hey."

"Ky."

Her jaw ticked, and he wondered if she filed away all the things that reminded her of him like he had. Maybe even her nickname.

"I thought you'd be at the shop," she said.

"Heading there later. You?"

She tucked her hands into the back pockets of her jeans, then crossed her arms, then dropped them to her side and shrugged, all of it meant to look like she didn't care, when really all it did was show that she was every bit as uncomfortable as him. "Ally's there now, so I took a break to grab us some lunch."

"Ah. She seems to be working out well."

"She is." Kylie eyed the register again. "I should probably." She motioned away, then, seeming to remember why she walked over, smiled at his mom again. "It's really good to see you, Mrs. Littleton."

Grace smiled in that way that said she understood far better than they did what was going on between them. "You too, dear. Don't be a stranger, okay?"

Kylie nodded. "Thank you, I won't." Then she shot Brady one more fleeting look before heading to the register, grabbing a bag waiting for her there, and taking off back out the door.

His mom sat back in her chair and crossed her arms. "If that's fine, then I'd hate to think what upset or confused or sad looks like on you these days."

Brady tracked Kylie as she walked down the sidewalk, her head down now. "Yeah…"

* * * *

Kylie couldn't stop walking. She dropped Ally's lunch at the shop, then told her she had something else to pick up, though she couldn't for the life of her think of what. All she knew was that she needed to keep walking. She needed to put some distance between her and the disaster she'd just suffered at AJ&P.

Of course, maybe it hadn't been such a disaster on the outside. On the inside, though, the whole place had exploded in every thought she'd had. Her palms had gone clammy and her heart was racing.

Seeing Mrs. Littleton was one thing. It was awkward, and she still felt guilty as all heck that she'd hurt her. That was the thing about a relationship like hers and Brady's—it wasn't just the two them that were involved. She loved the Littletons, even his brothers, so it had all but broken her all over again to leave without saying good-bye to them. But Brady had been clear back then.

Still, she could have survived seeing Mrs. Littleton alone. Throw Brady into the mix, the two of them, the woman who had been every bit of the mother she'd always wanted and that her own mother would never be. And then the man she once thought she'd spend the rest of her life with. It was too much. She'd wanted to laugh it off or scream or, hell, cry, but she couldn't do anything but stand there in misery, all the emotions pent up inside her.

So now she was walking in hopes of working them off.

The day was beautiful, a slight chill in the air like it might snow any second, even though it was only the middle of November. The trees had already lost most of their leaves, and the street posts were already decorated for Christmas with greenery and lights. It all made her wish for a do-over or a get out of jail free card or something that could free her from the guilt and the anger and the pain.

Now, looking back, it seemed like they could have talked through it all, but then Brady had to go be Brady and she was too stubborn to forgive him and then the rest was history.

Shaking her head to clear the thought, Kylie turned left down the next street and spotted a setup of Christmas trees, Fraser firs and Douglas firs, all bright green and full and calling to her. The shop already had three trees, but they were all artificial. What they needed was a real tree, with its amazing smell, to remind everyone who walked into the shop that it was Christmas.

An older man was setting up another tree when she walked up.

"Hi there, can you tell me how much these cost?"

His thick gray brow furrowed and he ran a hand over his nearly bald head. "Well now that depends on the size and type you choose."

"Okay, how about that one," Kylie said, pointing to the one he was holding. It was a little on the tall side, but she thought she could have him trim a little off the stem and then she could nix the star on top. It'd be fine.

"This one?" He eyed the tree like he'd just remembered that he was holding it. "I'd say sixty would be fine."

Kylie unzipped her purse and rummaged through the pockets until she felt for the wad of cash she'd shoved in there the day before. She pulled it out and counted it out, then cringed. "I have fifty."

The man glanced around, then smiled at her. "It'll be our little secret."

"Really? Thank you. Thank you so much." She hugged him lightly, passed over the fifty dollars, then took the tree and started dragging it away.

"Wait, miss. Don't you want me to wrap it up? Help you get it to your car? Well, a tree that size, I hope you have a truck."

In all the excitement of choosing the tree, Kylie hadn't considered actually getting it to the shop. She adjusted it in her grasp, tried to lift it a little, and yeah, that wasn't happening.

"Actually, you know, I'm pretty close to here. I think I can just figure it out."

The man's eyebrows lifted. "If you're sure."

"I'm good. Thank you again." She smiled as she reached the end of the street and started toward Merrily Christmas, only the tree was four times as wide as she was and several feet taller than her five-two self.

The tree swayed and she swayed with it, then widened her stance to steady it. "Woah boy." Then her eyes locked with someone down the sidewalk, his arms crossed, a giant grin on his face.

"Need some help?" Brady called.

Kylie frowned. "No. I'm good." She moved around to try to gain control of the tree again, only to lose her grip and then grab it before it hit the sidewalk. "Crap."

Several people peeked out from their store windows and Kylie waved to them that all was okay, until she realized that she needed both hands on the giant tree if she hoped to keep it from falling.

She started to drag it again, when strong arms reached around her, pinning her between him and the tree.

Brady's hands locked on the tree. "I've got it." He stood it up tall, then released one of his arms so she could step out.

Kylie fought back the annoyance creeping up her neck. "I told you that I have it."

"Yet you were about to face death by tree limbs. Why are you being so stubborn?"

"I…" The truth was she didn't know. She just knew that Brady helping her felt a little like admitting she was wrong, and she couldn't do that. Not then and not now. "Not stubborn. I just don't want you to pull a muscle or anything. You know, hurt your chances of finishing your build." She thought about it, pressed a finger to her lip and tapped slowly. "Come to think of it, maybe I do want you to pull a muscle. Here." She released the tree, expecting it to sway as it would have with her if she were holding it by one hand, but it didn't budge an inch.

Brady flashed her a cocky grin and flexed his bicep. "This baby's not going anywhere."

Stupid muscles. Kylie pursed her lips.

"And I'm happy to use them to help you get it to the shop, so long as you ask me nicely."

There it was—the real reason Brady came over. Not to be nice, but to embarrass her. He wanted to show that she needed him so she would have to admit that she wasn't as self-sufficient as she claimed.

"I know what you're doing."

His eyebrows rose. "I believe it's called helping you."

"Helping me?"

"Or you could call it saving your ass, whatever you like."

Anger pricked in her chest, rising up in that way it had her entire life. Her best friend back in South Carolina, Taryn, used to tell her that she was a tiny bomb ready to explode at a given notice. She always hated it when Taryn said that, but she couldn't deny there was some accuracy there.

"You're trying to get me to admit that I can't do it on my own, that I'm not self-sufficient, independent, whatever. That I need you."

"You do need me."

The anger sparked. "Are you insane? I bought this thing on my own, dragged it all the way here. I can get it to the shop. I don't need you."

He sighed loudly. "You really are a piece of work, aren't you? I came here to help you before you and the tree face-planted on the sidewalk, and you can't even say thank you. You can't even ask me to help you get it back to the shop, despite the fact that you know you need me to help you." He shook his head. "Guess some things don't change," he muttered under his breath, and that did it. The paper-thin wall holding back Kylie's anger exploded.

"Yeah, I guess some things don't change. Here I am trying to save Franny's shop, and here you are thinking of yourself first and trying to take it. I told you that I didn't need your help, but you refused to leave me alone. I don't need a hero. I didn't then and I don't now." The words were out too quickly for Kylie to think them through, and instantly she wished she could take them back.

Brady went still, his eyes on her like he was trying to work through the disaster before him, before they slanted into slits, and before she could say another word, he lifted the tree up with both hands and started toward the shop.

Several people had walked out from their shops to take in the commotion, and Kylie had enough good sense to plant a smile on her face in hopes of faking that it was all a joke. But there was no pretending here. Anger radiated between them, building and building until it was a wonder they didn't fight for control of the tree.

"You're impossible."

"Yeah, well, you're not exactly a peach yourself."

"I said I had it."

"I didn't ask. Now get the door."

Gritting her teeth, Kylie grabbed the handle and threw it open so hard it slammed against the doorjamb. "After you," she said, motioning forward.

He grinned at her, no hint of the anger she'd seen before on his face. "Ah, see, you can be sweet. Who knew?" He went on into the shop, leaving her sputtering behind him.

"You need a stand."

"No kidding, Sherlock. I have one." She motioned to the stand she'd placed by the register that morning. At the time, she'd intended to see if Ally wanted it, but then the tree tent thing was there and the rest was history.

Brady dropped it into the stand and tightened the screws into the trunk. "Where do you want it? I'm guessing by the large window? Yeah, that'll look best. I'll put it there." He moved before she could respond, and sure enough, it was the best place for the tree, but that didn't mean she wanted him making the call.

"Any other decisions you want to make on my behalf? Should I invite you over to pick out my clothes in the morning?"

His lips quirked up. "Is that an invitation to see you undressed? 'Cause been there, done that. Have the virgin card still in my wallet."

Kylie froze, her cheeks burning in humiliation as the words cut through her chest and into her heart. "Seriously?"

He took a step back, his eyes on the ground, then over to Franny, who had stood up behind the counter, a clear look of disapproval on her face. "I'll just…" He nodded to his side of the shop, and Kylie focused on her tree, unwilling to look at Franny as she neared.

"You okay?"

Her lip trembled, but she clamped down on that sucker instead of allowing it to shake the rest of her. "Peachy."

"If you want me to go back on what we agreed to, if it's too much…"

Kylie rolled her shoulders back and smiled at her godmother. "No, it's fine. I just need to get a little smarter around him, that's all."

Franny ran a hand over Kylie's hair, smoothing it back. "Well see, that's the problem with being around someone who knows you deep in your bones. Your bones might lengthen and grow, they might even break from time to time. But they're still *your* bones, individual to you, that part doesn't change."

A moment passed, sadness creeping in at the realization that only two people in the world knew her deep down, deep in the bones as Franny said, and one of them just spoke as though all they had was nothing more than a virgin card eager to be picked up and then forgotten.

"You know if you cry I'll have to kill him," a voice called from behind them, and Franny and Kylie both turned to find Ally standing there, hands on her hips, her face full of sass. They all laughed, until her phone chirped from her back pocket and she jerked it out, her fingers moving at warp speed. "Come on, baby. Just one. Mama just needs one."

Kylie leaned in closer. "The Real N Feel doll?"

"Yes," Ally said. "And Walmart has one!" Her eyes flashed as she went to work pulling up the Walmart app on her phone and cycling through to find the toy. All three women stared down at her iPhone with bated breath as the toy loaded on the screen. Only to show all five versions with a giant OUT OF STOCK beside them. Ally's shoulders slumped. "I'm never going to find this thing, and then Rena is going to be in tears on Christmas morning and it's all going to be my fault because I didn't know in July that this thing was going to be the hot toy. Who could have known? And why didn't the stupid manufacturer make more for the season? Seriously, how can you run out of supply before Christmas? It's every parent's nightmare."

Kylie gripped her shoulder. "We'll find one."

"You're sweet, but there's a greater chance of me sprouting wings and flying than tracking down one of these."

"Now, now, don't lose faith yet," Franny said. "We can all keep a lookout."

Ally offered a half smile, but it was obvious she had her doubts. "Well, if it's okay with you two, I think I'll head on to check a few stores before going home. Just to see."

"Of course, go. I'm going on home, too," Franny said. "Are you okay to close up?" she asked Kylie.

"I'm on it."

The two women gathered up their things, and Franny paused beside her on her way out. "Will you be long?"

"No. I'm going to work on this tree a little and then grab some takeout. Do you want anything?"

Franny shook her head. "No, I'll grab something at home." She kissed her cheek and headed out. Kylie locked the door behind her and turned their wooden OPEN sign around to CLOSED.

Clicking off the front lights, she turned around to find the Christmas lights on the two other trees providing a peaceful glow to the room. It wasn't until Brady walked in from the back that she realized he was still there.

"Hey," he said, his voice low. "Thought everyone left."

Kylie shrugged, her chest still tight from what he'd said. Why couldn't this be easier? Why couldn't these feelings swirling around in her chest just go away? "I wanted to decorate the new tree so it would be up for tomorrow since I'll be in a little late."

"Why will you be in late?" The question came quickly and a little too naturally for Kylie's taste. Like they were still something more than strangers.

"Ally is trying to find this toy on her daughter Rena's Christmas list, and it's sold out everywhere. Apparently Target gets a supply several times a week, but only a couple and no one knows which days they will receive them. Her husband works long hours with the electric company so he can't go wait in line to see if he can get one, and she can't leave Rena. I thought I'd go try for her."

Night had set in outside, chill seeping in to the shop. It reminded her so much of Christmases when she was little that she almost closed her eyes to bask in it for a moment.

She realized Brady was staring at her with a quizzical expression on his face. "It's going to be twenty degrees tomorrow morning, probably colder with the wind chill. Why would you suffer through that for a kid that isn't even yours?"

Kylie walked over to the counter, opened the bottom drawer and pulled out a fresh box of white lights, then a second and third because one was never enough. She opened each box, her thoughts inward as she thought about the question.

"Did you decide to ignore me?"

"No. I'm just not sure how to explain it." Connecting each set of lights, she plugged them into a nearby outlet to make sure they all worked. The lights brightened the shadowed space. She'd been lucky—so far, all of her lights had worked.

Brady approached and took the other end of the lights. "I can help you thread them around the tree if you would like. It's a tall tree." Kylie waved toward her step stool, but Brady piped in before she could mention it. "I know you don't need me to help, but I'd like to if it's okay with you. It's been a long time since I decorated a tree."

Their eyes met, and Kylie's resolve wavered. "Okay."

"So the question—do you have a freezing fetish or something?"

She laughed, the feel of it strange around Brady, this person who made her want to scream and cry in alternating succession every time she was around him. "It's hard to explain. It's just…I saw how desperate Ally was to get this for her little girl. It's the only thing on her Christmas list. I guess I just want to be a part of the magic of her getting her one true wish for Christmas."

Brady paused mid-motion to draping the lights around the tree, glanced at her. "You're going to freeze to help make her Christmas?"

"It's a small price to pay, don't you think?"

He went back to draping the lights, careful to push them into the limbs, threading in and out to get the look just right. "No, but then I never had your heart."

Actually, Kylie thought, *you did. You just never realized it.*

"Seems like if you give like that," he continued, "how can you guarantee the kid even appreciates it? He might not even play with it on Christmas morning and then all your aggravation was for nothing."

Kylie smiled. "First, *she* not he. And second, don't you remember Christmas morning and wanting that one special, perfect gift? There's no chance she won't play with it. But there is a chance that she will be devastated and sad if she doesn't get it. Then you take the risk of her no longer believing in Santa because she didn't get the present she wanted most. I have to help prevent that."

His gaze dropped to her again. "The American Girl doll thing?"

Kylie walked away to grab a box of vintage ornaments that she'd picked out for the tree. They were all gold and paper and looked like something you'd find in the fifties. She loved them.

"No, I just want to help. It's not about me."

Though that wasn't one hundred percent true. She did want to help, but she wanted to help because she knew what it was like to not get that special present you always wanted. It was her seventh Christmas and all she wanted in the world was an American Girl doll—Samantha. She was beautiful and came with a book about her life and every one of Kylie's friends had an American Girl doll. She wanted one, too. Her birthday came and went without getting the doll, despite the fact that her parents could easily afford it. They each drove luxury cars and wore nice clothes, though in truth Kylie discovered that was all a farce. They pretended to have money while actually spending every dollar they had…on themselves.

So that Christmas, she thought she had found the fix—Santa. Her mom took her that year with one of her friends and her daughter. Of course, the two women just wanted to shop at the mall, but they dropped the girls in line with Santa, and when it was Kylie's turn, she pronounced with perfect annunciation so there was no confusion—Samantha, the American Girl doll.

She went to sleep that night feeling hopeful. Santa would deliver. Santa would make sure that she received what her parents didn't give her.

But then Christmas morning came and she rushed downstairs to find four presents under the tree, each far too small to be a doll. She opened them slowly, praying some miracle would happen, but she ended up receiving bracelets and clothes and pretend makeup, stuff she had no interest in.

When tears filled her eyes, her mother laughed and said she was too old for dolls and then revealed the truth—there was no Santa. She'd spent the rest of the day in her room crying, and it stayed with her all her life.

So, yeah, maybe a tiny part of her wanted to do this because she would never wish that hurt on anyone, certainly not an innocent four-year-old whose mother genuinely cared but simply didn't have the time or resources to make it happen.

Kylie brought the box back around to the tree as Brady finished the lights. She started decorating in the way Franny had taught her all those years ago—creating a diamond shape with ornaments over and over until the tree was full.

"You know it wasn't you, right?"

Pausing with a bright red stuffed bird in her hand that was made of mixed patterns, she glanced over. "What wasn't?" Her heart went still, curiosity swirling. Maybe he was finally ready to admit that he was wrong, that he should have respected the way she was and not pushed.

Instead he said, "The Christmas thing, the birthdays thing. It was them, not you. You deserved to get the presents you wanted and to have a loving childhood. That was on them to deliver it. You did nothing wrong."

Tears pricked her eyes and she swallowed hard, trying to push away the swell of emotions. It had been a long time since she talked about her childhood, and even longer since she allowed herself to feel any hurt about it. After all, she wasn't abused. She wasn't yelled at repeatedly. She was just ignored—invisible. There were far worse things in life.

"I know." She placed the bird on a tree limb and continued decorating in silence, her thoughts growing darker and darker until finally Brady changed the subject.

"So what is the fancy toy anyway? A doll that pees or something?"

She laughed, the feel of it cutting through the storm clouds in her heart. Brady always had a way of making light of the darkest of moments. "Ally said it's like a robotic doll. They have boy and girl versions, and they can be trained to talk and walk and, hell, maybe clean your house for all I know." She laughed again, her thoughts of her parents pushed to the corner of her mind again, where they would forever live, fresh enough to pop up whenever they like but shadowed by the rigors of life so she could forget on occasion.

"Damn, that's a thing? Maybe I should get one."

"Good luck with that! Ally's on all these alert sites that ping her phone every time one comes into stock online, but then they're gone as soon as we get there. Then there are these hoarders who bought them all up early in the season and are now selling them on eBay for a fortune. It's ridiculous. The only hope Rena, her daughter, has is if she finds one at a store, but there are lines at Target hours before they open, only to find the store received one or two or sometimes none at all."

"That's crazy." Brady walked around her and took one of the ornaments from the box, then stopped. "Okay if I help?"

She smirked. "Do you remember how? You said it's been a long time since you decorated a tree. No woman in your life to show you the way?" The question was out before she thought better of it, or how badly she did not want to hear the answer.

He went around to the side of the tree, careful to continue the diamond pattern Kylie had started there. "No, no one I'd decorate a tree with." His eyes drifted over to her. "You?"

She shook her head. "No."

He nodded slowly.

"You cut your hair," she said, again wishing her spitfire mouth would keep quiet, but with no one around, the lights from the tree dimming the intensity of everything, she felt too comfortable. Like she had when they were together.

"About a year ago. Couldn't handle…" He trailed off as he grabbed another ornament, this one a small nutcracker with a trumpet.

"Couldn't handle brushing it?"

"You don't want to hear this stuff."

She couldn't decide if she did or didn't. It depended upon what he was going to say. "Go on, it's fine. A girlfriend wanted you to cut it?"

It was hard for Kylie to imagine. When they were together, she used to love to run her fingers through it. He used to get bad migraines when they were teens, and she would stroke his hair to soothe them away.

Brady stopped beside her, forcing her to look up. "No, she liked it. Most of the women I dated liked it. I didn't like them touching it. Every time one of them ran their fingers through my hair it would remind me how much I wished she were…" He paused.

"Wished she were?"

He released a breath. "You."

"Brady…"

He pulled back, his eyes on anything but her. "I really should get going."

"Brady," Kylie called, but he was already across the room now, once again putting space between them.

"See you tomorrow."

Chapter 6

Brady needed a beer. Stat. Hell, at this point, he needed a case. He needed to forget all the things his brain refused to forget and stop feeling all the things his heart refused to stop feeling. Being around Kylie brought out all the draw and attraction he'd had for her from the beginning. How could years pass, and yet that feeling remain?

It had taken a long and insane amount of time for him to figure out how to breathe again after Kylie left. It was strange how someone could become such an ingrained part of your soul that once they were gone, you no longer knew how to be you. But that was what had happened—he forgot how to be Brady.

He pulled into his garage and walked inside his too-nice house, dropped his keys on the kitchen countertop, and pulled a beer out of the fridge. Cracking open the can, he took a long pull and his gaze landed on his Keurig. It felt like years ago that Kylie had walked in here that night and all but demanded they share the business. Now, he found himself wishing she would stop by and actually have coffee with him. Even if she didn't speak, even if she yelled at him. Just the thought of her being here, in his space, made him happy.

And that was part of the problem.

She had walked back into town and taken up her previous residence in his heart, all without his permission.

With a long exhale, he grabbed his phone and scrolled through until he found Kylie's number, and then, before he could chicken out, he hit call. He grabbed his beer and went on into his bedroom, the only room in the house that felt like him.

The phone rang several times before finally going to voicemail, and his heart clenched before he tossed the phone onto his bed. It was probably for the best, but he couldn't deny that it hurt to think she was screening.

Setting down his beer on his nightstand, he turned around, torn between a shower he didn't really want to take and going to sleep even though he wasn't tired. That was when his gaze caught on the painting over his bed, and once again, his heart contracted.

He'd put everything away that had anything at all to do with Kylie... except that painting.

They'd known each other a long time, but it wasn't until that one art class in high school that things changed. They were assigned seats beside each other, partnered numerous times. He was the classic jock and she was the classic nerd, and yet every time she laughed he became transfixed. It had taken him a surprisingly short amount of time for him to fall in love with her, but the moment he knew was when she was working on that painting.

The painting was of a tiny boat caught in a storm in the middle of the ocean. Forever she would paint these happy scenes, all bright and airy, but that day she came in and worked tirelessly on the stormy ocean scene. He found her there later that evening, after hours, when the art lab was open for finishing projects. He walked in and found her still working on the tiny boat in the middle of the ocean. Every detail about the sky, the waves, the rain, was intricate and lifelike. But the boat itself was blurry, nothing defined, everything about it forgettable. It was then she told him that it was her birthday. He asked if she was going out with her parents or if they were waiting on her, and she had simply said, "They didn't remember."

Brady had all but dragged her to the only decent pizza place in town, and they'd spent the night playing in the small arcade there and eating more pizza than either should ingest in a lifetime. It had been one of the best days of his life. He had asked for the painting, and with reluctance, she gave it to him.

Forever he viewed the boat as her, but then she left and he felt the world spinning around him, the pain so real he thought it would kill him. It was then his view changed and he saw it as himself. The painting carried from place to place with him—to college, his first job, and all the moves after that one, and then finally when he landed back in Crestler's Key after his father's heart attack and after Zac returned.

Well, there would be no sleep now for sure, so he finished off his beer and went on into his bathroom to take a shower and hopefully clear his thoughts.

He turned on the water and let it run to heat up to the desired scorching he preferred, then he undressed and stepped inside, allowing the hot water to cover him and ease some of his thoughts. Immediately, he regretted calling Kylie and thought through some excuses—accidental call? Question about the shop? He would need to come up with something before tomorrow.

Stepping out of the shower, he toweled off and went on into his room and threw on pajama pants. He picked up his phone to put it on the charger and froze at the missed call.

Kylie. Maybe she hadn't screened after all.

He eyed the time, then hit call, once again too eager to hear her voice to let his fear stop him. She answered on the second ring.

"Hey," she said.

He bit his lip. "Hey."

"I had a missed call from you. It was probably an accident or something. I call people by mistake all the time and it's always the most random people and at the most random of times. So I'm sure it was—"

"It wasn't an accident."

She released a breath into the phone, and Brady closed his eyes.

"Did you need to talk about something at the shop?" she asked, her voice lower now.

Brady sat down on his bed and leaned back against his pillows. "No."

"Right."

"Would you rather I not call you?" he asked.

She paused and he feared that his heart was about to take another beating, when she said. "No."

"I'm sure you want to know why I called, but I don't know. I just..."

"Needed to?"

"Yeah."

Brady drew a long breath and released slowly. "Yeah."

"Want to hear a confession?"

He contemplated whether he did or not. She could confess that she didn't want to talk to him, that it bothered her, and then what? But he was never the kind of guy to let fear dictate his actions, so instead he said, "Shoot."

"I almost called you last night. It was raining again and bits of sleet mixed in and I thought we might get our first snow. I don't know, it just made me think about...well, anyway."

A slow smile curled his lips. "Made you think about Fowler Park?"

She laughed. "Yes. It was so cold and everyone went out there for that Thanksgiving celebration thing with the bands and food, but everyone left early because it was so cold. So, we ended up..."

"Dancing all by ourselves while the band glared at us because they wanted to leave."

"And then it started snowing. Just small flakes at first, and then huge ones. We rarely got snow in November, but there it was. It was a good day."

"Yeah…it was." Brady padded out of his room, opened his fridge and grabbed another beer. He'd need more liquid courage to survive this conversation. He went back to his room and sat down on the bed again, cracked the beer, and took a sip.

"What are you doing?" Kylie asked, her voice low again, almost a whisper.

He thought about the question and how weird this whole conversation felt. Like something out of their past. Like something binding the past to the future. "I'm sitting in bed, drinking a beer, talking to a pretty girl and wondering why the hell she's talking back to me. Kind of reminds me of the first time you called me."

"Me? I didn't call you. You called me."

He laughed loudly. "Still as stubborn as ever. No, sweetheart, it was you all the way. It was a week after that pizza date on your birthday and I was going out of my freakin' mind. Then you called and acted all like you had some question about art, when I knew shit about it." He chuckled again. "You never wanted to like me, but you couldn't help it. I had mad charm back then."

Silence filled the space, and he worried that this walk down memory lane was too much for her. It was too much for him, too. "You did. Though I think you have more now."

Goose bumps spread across his skin at the compliment, and he worried that he was walking down a road that was sure to come to a dead end and leave him lost and alone.

"Ky…"

"Can we not talk about that tonight? Can we just pretend?"

Brady stared out into his room, that inner need of his to fix whatever was wrong before moving forward so great that he almost said no, they needed to talk about it. But he'd made the mistake of pushing too hard last time, and look where that left him. Broken and without her. And though he didn't know what was happening right now, probably nothing at all, he didn't want it to end. Maybe they would only have this one call and go back to despising each other tomorrow. But for tonight, yeah, he could pretend that everything was fine and normal.

He pushed under his covers and slumped down, clicked off his lamp and allowed darkness to surround him. "Whatever you need." The last time, he'd been so sure of them that he hadn't considered what she needed. Only what they needed, or really what he needed. He was older now, and he hoped with that age a bit more selfless.

"How are you liking being back?" he asked.

But she didn't answer.

"Ky?"

The sound of sniffling met his ears and his chest tightened.

"I am sorry."

Swallowing hard, he tried to push away the memory of her walking away. And the memory of him not going after her. Not begging her to try, to work things out. Of not telling her that she was the most important thing in the world to him, because now he knew that had been the problem—she had never been number one to anyone. Why couldn't he have seen that she would back away at the fear that she'd dropped to number two on his list?

He tried to draw a breath again, but the ache in his chest made it hard.

"Yeah...me, too."

Chapter 7

Kylie woke the next morning with a smile on her face, a fresh attitude, and a giant desire to succeed. At first, she thought the call the night before had been a dream, but then she glanced at her phone and scrolled until she saw Brady's name there. It was real. She had talked with her ex for over an hour, until they were both too tired to keep going, the call about nothing at all, and yet it was everything.

She showered quickly and got dressed, dotted a bit of concealer under her eyes, swiped blush on her cheeks and applied mascara. Then she swiped her trusty Lip Smacker Dr. Pepper lip balm on her lips and went on downstairs to grab some coffee. Franny wasn't awake yet, which was unusual, but it was only six a.m.

Turning on the coffee maker, she waited for it to brew, then searched for directions to the Target she intended to stake out that morning for Rena's toy. All she needed was to leave a note for Franny so she could open the shop.

Hopefully, if everything went as planned, Kylie would have the goods in hand by eight when the store opened and then she would be back to Merrily Christmas by nine. Easy peasy.

The smell of fresh coffee filled the room, and Kylie drew a long breath. It had been a long time since she'd felt this hopeful about life, and she intended to build on it. Today she would score Rena's toy. Today she would post the list of weekly activities at the shop. Today she would see Brady.

The giddiness in her stomach was almost too much, though she told herself to take things slow. They had one night of decorating a tree and one phone call. Neither equaled happily ever after.

"You're up early."

Kylie jumped and spun around to find Franny in the doorway. She looked tired, her general uplifting spirit darker.

"Are you feeling okay?"

Franny waved her off. "Yeah, just didn't sleep much last night. I'm good. Where are you off to?"

Kylie made her godmother some coffee and helped her sit at the kitchen table, which earned her an annoyed look.

"I'm old, not dead."

"I know," Kylie said. "Doesn't mean you don't need some help from time to time."

Franny took a sip of her coffee instead of answering. "Where are you going? Or are you going to make me guess?"

"I'm going to Target to see if they have any of those toys Ally wants."

"It's six a.m. The store doesn't open until eight. You'll be there by seven, maybe earlier. You're going to sit outside?"

"I've got gloves and a beanie and I just bought that North Face down coat. It'll be a good excuse to test it out."

Her eyebrows lifted. "Is this about the American Girl doll?"

Damn, why does everyone have to bring that thing up? "No. It's about me helping a little girl's Christmas wish come true."

"It's about the American Girl doll," Franny muttered. "I still don't know why you never asked me for it. You know I would have bought it for you."

"I know." But the truth was she never asked her for anything. She loved Franny so much and Franny loved her so much that she was afraid to be too needy. Consequently, she never asked Franny for anything and instead appreciated every single thing the woman ever bought her.

"Your parents did a number on you with that thing."

"I don't know why all of you are focused on that thing. I'm over that. It's not about the doll."

Franny lifted her head. "Wait. All of who?"

And now it was time to go. "No one. Just, Brady might have mentioned it yesterday."

The smile that split Franny's face could have lit the whole town. "I see. And how is Brady these days? Cute as a button, that's for sure. Some men just age well. He's definitely one of them, wouldn't you say?"

Um, yes. Yes, she would definitely say. But not to her godmother. She thought of what Brady had said at the shop about cutting his hair because he didn't want anyone else running her hands through it. It sounded a little like maybe, just maybe, he wasn't over her. And then he called her. *He* called *her*. Surely that meant something, right? Or maybe it was nothing and she was getting her hopes up and—

"Ky."

"Hm?" she asked as she screwed on the cap to her Yeti mug.

"Be careful, okay?"

"I will. It's less than an hour away."

"Not with the ride. With Brady."

Kylie shook her head. "I'm not going to get hurt."

The smile returned to Franny's face. "Actually, I meant be careful with him."

That threw her. "What do you mean?"

"You know your issues, child. He knows your issues. You don't mean to pull back, but those parents of yours did more damage than just forgetting to get you a doll you wanted. He's a good man. Be careful."

Kylie went numb as she took in her godmother's face. Had it really all been Kylie's fault?

"Trust me, it's not like that. We're just...well, I don't know what. But not that."

"Whatever you say."

Franny turned on the TV to watch the morning weather and Kylie grabbed her coffee and keys. "See you at the shop. Hopefully with the goods in hand."

But as Kylie slipped into her car and turned on the heat, she no longer felt so hopeful. If it was all her, her unwillingness to compromise, her fears destroying what they had, then how would they ever find a way back to good?

Needing a distraction, she turned on Christmas music and started on her journey to Target. "Jingle Bell Rock" filled the car, and she sang along as she drove, thankful that traffic wasn't a problem at the early hour. With any luck, she would get there, grab the toy, and leave without much of an issue. Maybe they even opened the store early for hot items like this, or handed out hot chocolate. Which, come to think of it, hot chocolate would make an excellent addition to her Meet Santa Day on Black Friday.

Kylie made a mental note to pick up some good hot chocolate mixes from Target while she was there, and half an hour later, she pulled into the lot. There were very few cars parked, causing that hope of hers to bloom. Until she parked the car, put on her gloves and beanie, and stepped out, only to stop dead in her tracks at the line stemming out from Target's door, lining the wall, and disappearing around the side.

There were people in foldout chairs, in sleeping bags, people wrapped in thick blankets. One guy even had some sort of battery operated heater that several others were crowded around. Kylie didn't even know they made such a thing. Her heart sank.

Frowning at her stupid fleece gloves, she made her way to the back of the line. It was seven in the morning! What were all of these people doing here and what time did they get here? Had they been there since the previous night? Surely not.

She leaned against the building, prepared to suffer for the good of Rena and her Christmas wish, when the couple in front of her turned around, their faces a bit too cheery for the hour and the cold and the lack of Target employees passing out hot chocolate. She'd need to put in a call when she left to recommend that for another day.

"Hi, I'm Rick, this is my wife, Nina. What are you waiting on?" the man asked, while Nina waved hello. "Doll or gaming console? That's Bree. She's here for the game," Rick said, pointing to a woman in front of him, who also turned around to wave. "But those three up there are for sure doll. We're guessing everyone else in line is a seventy-thirty mix, with the majority here for the doll. I hear they're going for three hundred on eBay now, but we haven't checked since we scored our last one."

"Last one?" Kylie asked, her eyebrows lifting. As far as she knew, these things were rarer than gold. How had they already secured one? And what did they plan to do with the second?

"Yes," Nina said. "We managed to get one a few weeks ago for our eldest daughter, but now our son is hoping for one, too, so here we are. This is the third time we've waited, and we've been watching the crowds. The trick is to alternate who waits in line and arrive super early. Then you walk up to join your group. Target lets each person buy one. The two women first in line are always here. They must have a dozen or more by now."

"Wait a second," Kylie said, waving her hands and instantly regretting it because now her hands were cold. "Why so many? Are they supplying for foster kids or something?"

Rick's face etched in anger. "No, they run Rare Treasures, the eBay shop. Been selling them for a fortune for weeks now."

"That's horrible. Why doesn't Target refuse to sell to them?"

Bree turned around to answer. "They can't, now can they? But at least they aren't as bad as Walmart. They allow their employees to buy them, so you don't even stand a chance there."

"How the heck are we supposed to get one of these with those odds?" Kylie asked, her chest heaving in aggravation.

"Girl, I know," Bree said. "My son put nothing else on his list. Just this. What am I supposed to say on Christmas morning?"

Kylie shook her head. "I know."

"Do you have a boy or girl?" Rick asked her.

"Me? Oh, neither. I'm here for a friend. She has a daughter, and my friend can't come wait in line, so here I am."

Nina placed her hand on her chest. "That's the sweetest thing I've ever heard. Must be a good friend for you to go to so much trouble."

Actually, Kylie barely knew Ally, but she couldn't bring herself to say that in front of these people, so she just nodded. "She is."

The line started to move, and Kylie checked her watch. It was only seven thirty. "What's going on?" she asked as grumbling from the front of the line started trickling back.

It was Rick who answered. "The store manager just came out and told the crowd that they only received two. Everyone's leaving now."

"Two?"

"The Rare Treasures team will get those two, so there's no point in staying."

Kylie rose onto her toes to peer around the building. "But maybe they miscounted or something. Maybe it's worth staying."

Bree and Nina both shook their heads. "No point. Trust us. They already opened all their boxes from their shipment. They only have the two."

"So then what do you do?"

"You try again tomorrow," Nina said.

"And it's supposed to be in the teens in the morning," Bree added.

Kylie followed the women toward the parking lot, her hands icy, her toes numb, and suddenly there was a new number one on her to-do list for the season.

She would find this doll.

* * * *

Brady opened the door to Merrily Christmas slash Southern Dive & ETC, the new name they'd given to the shop, for his brothers. It had taken him weeks to get his side of the shop organized in the way he wanted without killing the Christmas vibe that Kylie and Franny needed for their shop. Finally, he'd decided to have a rustic, wooden counter in the center, a giant trophy fish on the wall behind it, and then shelves on either side with bait, hooks, and all the goods that an angler might need, whether he was heading out to salt or fresh water. Then Brady had the rest of his stock and all packaging in the back.

Kylie had agreed to give him extra workspace if he agreed to allow her to use the tables whenever she needed to wrap gifts. It worked out, and already he had solid foot traffic coming in to buy this or that.

Zac and Charlie paused in the middle of the shop, one facing Southern Dive's side, the other Merrily. Charlie was the first to ask "And whose idea was this again? Why not just buy the whole shop? Where you going to put the rods when they deliver?"

The brothers had enough requests for specialty rods and reels that they'd decided to expand their collection. Again.

"We talked about this," Brady said, fighting the annoyance he felt. Why couldn't they ever just go along with what he said or did? Why was it always a battle or a surge of questions? "This was we make half the investment and still have everything we need. And when the Christmas shop fails, we'll get the rest of the building for a steal. It's smart business."

Zac turned around to face him now. "And what if it doesn't fail? Are you prepared to do what you have to do here? Without feelings involved?"

At that moment, Kylie walked in the main door, her cheeks bright red, her eyes glassy. Her entire body was tensed up, and she was dressed like she'd just hiked through a blizzard.

"Sure, no problem," Brady said, distracted. "Hey, y'all heading back over to the other building? I'll come over in a bit."

"Brady, we need to talk about this."

"We will," he said, half there, half already to Kylie. "Later."

"What about the rods?" Charlie called after him.

Brady waved through the air nonchalantly. "Delivering on Monday. I've got it. Promise."

He knew they were watching him, not at all confident in what he said, but they could go screw themselves. He would handle business, and if push came to shove, he would buy the rest of the building and put Franny out of business. He could do that, would do that. Somehow.

"Hey there," he said as he approached Kylie. "Didn't realize the snowman look was the trend these days."

She shot him her trademark you're-about-as-funny-as-dirt look, and he smiled still brighter. "You know, I think I liked it better when we weren't really talking."

"Now, now, you know you don't mean that."

"No, I don't," she said, her eyes meeting his, and for a second, he was lost there, swimming in a sea of blue, wondering how he was going to pull himself away and find air again.

Clearing his throat, he forced himself to look away. "So, what's the story here. Car trouble or something?"

"No. Toy trouble."

Brady eyed her. "You didn't."

"I did."

"Damn. How long did you wait and where?"

Kylie rubbed her hands together, but she didn't remove her gloves. He fought the urge to take her hands in his and warm them himself. "About an hour at Target. Only to find out the stupid store only received two. Which, according to Rick, Nina, and Bree, went to the stupid Rare Treasures team of chicks that show up every morning at the crack of dawn to buy the dolls all up and then sell them for five times the price in the eBay store."

"You're joking? And who are Rick, Nina, and Bree?"

She busied herself with trying to remove her gloves. "You know, just the regulars that go there every day to try to get one for their kids."

"You befriended the regulars? Of course you did." He bit his lip as he stared down at her frozen fingers trying to work off her gloves, before deciding he couldn't watch the mess any longer. It was like watching a dog chasing its tail.

He grabbed her hands and eased the gloves off each, then closed her hands together and rubbed them between his. "Dang, you are freezing. Let's get you some coffee."

But she had stopped moving and was staring at him, her body trembling slightly, yet he had a feeling it was less to do with the cold and more to do with the fact that they were touching. A decade had passed, and he was back here, taking her in and making her a part of his world again. He needed to take a step back, needed to go back to his side of the shop and find his brain, but he couldn't make himself move.

"Hey, B-man, need to see you for a second."

Brady drew a slow breath at the old nickname and glanced over his shoulder to find both his brothers still there, both still watching him. Both still judging him. "Right." He blew onto Kylie's hands and then rubbed them again. "Go grab coffee. I set up a Keurig in the back and stocked it with k-cups. There's some travel cups under the counter where it's sitting. Take whatever you need."

"You didn't have to do that," she said.

"I know, but your coffee maker was trash. Couldn't go all day without good coffee. Now go get you a cup. Grab me one while you're at it," he said with a wink, then walked over to his brothers, each step locking up his heart and creating that solid armor he wore whenever he was around anyone but Kylie. If only he could find a way to wear it around her, too, then maybe he could have saved himself the last time. Maybe he could save himself this time.

"What?" he asked once Kylie went to the back.

Charlie wasn't looking at him, which meant he was going to force Zac to say it.

"What the hell is going on here?" Zac asked, never one to beat around the bush.

"What are you talking about? And can you hurry up with it? I'm slammed here. I don't have time to guess what's going through your head."

"Yeah, you look super busy," Charlie said, facing him now. "Just not in the way we thought."

"What is that supposed to mean? Seriously, what is with you, two? I thought you'd be excited to see all the progress. I have this place operational, and in no time at all. What did you expect here? Oh, right, not like I'd ever meet your damn expectations, right?"

Zac threw up his hands then. "All right, stop. We're not trying to fight. The shop looks great, and we all agreed to move forward with the plan to buy half now, half later. We're good there. It's not the shop we're worried about—it's you."

"There's nothing to worry about with me. I'm good."

Charlie nodded slowly. "Right, so why are you staring at that door?" He pointed at the door to the back, the door Kylie had disappeared through and hadn't yet returned. Brady didn't even realize he was staring at it until Charlie mentioned it. Maybe he wasn't so good and fine after all. But he couldn't admit that to them.

"I'm not," he said, focusing on his brothers. "Now if there's nothing else..."

"Tread carefully, little brother." Charlie was never as forceful with his opinions as Zac. For him to be giving them now meant he was worried, and he was always the one in the family to do the shrink thing and help each of them through their crap. He knew more than anyone what had been in Brady's head after Kylie left—how dark he'd gone and long it had taken him to come back to the light.

"I've got this under control."

Kylie appeared then and instantly Brady glanced over, his heart picking up speed, the desire to check on her so great he thought he was losing his mind. Maybe he was.

"Clearly," Zac said, and Brady shot him a look.

"You need anything else? Or you going to just stand here and interpret every move I make all day?"

"Nah, I'll leave that for Ms. Franny. Seeing as how she's staring between the two of you like she's already got you figured out."

Brady turned around to find Franny watching him with that sad puppy expression that so many wore around him in those first few days and weeks, once he showed his face.

"Yeah, anyway, I've got some inventory to unpack. See y'all at Mom and Dad's for dinner tonight."

He walked off before his brothers could ask anything else. Now to figure out how to get out of dinner so he wouldn't have to face the twenty-twenty twice in one day.

Brady went to the back, then, realizing he needed more distance, pushed on out the back door and outside. Chilly wind hit him immediately, and he embraced it, letting himself feel the cold so he wouldn't have to think about everything his brothers had said. And how right they'd been.

He shivered beneath his fleece pullover, but he allowed himself another minute to clear his head before going back inside, only to find Franny standing there, waiting on him.

"Hi," he said. "You okay?"

She laughed. "Funny, I was about to ask you the same thing."

Brady ran a hand over his head. "Seems to be a popular question these days."

"I'm betting your answer could stop the questions. Assuming it's that you're being smart about this, taking it slow, and keeping your head on straight."

Brady cocked a grin. "Y'all are all talking like I'm the woman in this situation. I'm the dude. The one who's detached and needs poking and shit. I'm not the one you need to worry about falling apart here."

But even as he said the words, he didn't believe them. And by the look on Franny's face, neither did she.

Franny gripped his arm and squeezed once. "All right then. I'll let you be."

She headed toward the back door and Brady opened it for her. "Heading out for the day?"

"Just a doctor's appointment. No big deal."

"Okay, feel free to call me if you need anything. You have my number, right?"

A smile curved her mouth. "I do indeed." She winked and continued on outside, leaving Brady alone once again.

Christmas music poured out from the shop, through the walls and doors, hitting his ears, and for the first time in a long time, he didn't wish someone would turn it off. Maybe he was insane for allowing himself to be open with Kylie, to take the risk of falling for her all over again, but wasn't it worth the risk to feel something rather than to go a lifetime feeling nothing at all?

The door to the shop opened, and Brady peered over.

"Thank God," Kylie said as she peeked her head around the door. "Annie-Jean down the street has agreed to supply cookie dough for that little cookie baking thing I brought in, but I can't decide on two flavors. Can you help?"

Brady set down the box he'd just lifted to open up, and walked over to her. "Sure. What do you have?"

"All right, so don't kill me, but it doesn't really help if you can see them. So…" She stepped out from behind the door, one hand behind her back, and stopped right in front of him, an uneasy expression on her face as she used her free hand to turn him around.

"Yeah, not loving having my back to you. Am I about to get covered in cookies instead of simply tasting them?"

Kylie laughed. "Hey, there are worse punishments, right? But no, just close your eyes okay?"

"And how exactly am I supposed to pick up a cookie and take a bite if I have my eyes closed?"

She pulled back as if it should be obvious. "Easy. I'm going to feed you."

Brady cocked an eyebrow. "You're going to feed me? Sounds a little kinky."

"It's cookies, for Christ's sake."

"Hey, sweetheart, you can call it whatever you like. Wouldn't be the first person I heard use food references."

"You talk like there have been a lot of them."

He continued to stare at her. "Would it bother you if I said there was?"

She didn't answer immediately, and the Christmas song changed, "Silent Night" starting up. With the smell of cookies wafting from behind her, that innocent look in her eyes, and Christmas all around them, Brady couldn't help thinking of how many kisses he'd stolen in this shop. How many times he pulled her behind a display or into the back, all for a soft kiss that never appeased him, yet he couldn't resist. She was an addiction he would never overcome, and just how deep that addiction ran in his bloodline became more and more apparent every time he was around her.

"So, the cookies?" he asked, because while he'd love nothing more than to stay here and ignore everything else, this was a one-man shop here for his end of it, and he was that one man.

Kylie cleared her throat. "Right. Cookies, which are not at all a metaphor for anything else," she said, then swallowed hard. "Okay, close your eyes."

Licking his lips once, Brady did as she asked, then lowered his head a bit so it was directed toward her. "Ready when you are."

The smell of freshly baked cookies hit his nose, and then he felt her fingertips graze his lips, and he fought the urge to groan.

"Open," she breathed.

Brady's heartbeat picked up speed, everything around him disappearing as all his senses honed in on her fingertips. He opened his mouth and she dropped the cookie bite in. It took every ounce of his control not to suck her fingertips in with the bite. This woman was going to be the death of him.

"So?" she asked, her voice a whisper, like she too felt the intensity of the moment. There couldn't be a foot between them, and no one around to watch. No one to see Brady lean into her.

"Oatmeal raisin."

"You like?"

"All will be revealed in the end," he said with a grin. "Bring on the next."

He licked his lips again to remove the cookie crumbs, and could have sworn he caught a sigh from Kylie before she said, "Option two." Her fingertips rested against his mouth again, and this time he opened without her having to ask. A bite dropped onto his tongue, and he closed his mouth and chewed, the cookie melting in chocolaty goodness. He moaned as he took in the flavor.

"I need another taste of that one. Just to be safe."

A giggle sounded from Kylie's direction and he smiled. "No way."

"Saving the rest for yourself?"

"You know it."

His grin spread. "All right, so that was double chocolate chip. An AJ&P specialty, and I already know it's gonna be my favorite."

"Now, now, I may just have a surprise for you. This is the last one."

Brady opened up, but this time, when Kylie dropped the bite inside, her finger lingered, and he closed his mouth around her finger, licking the tip before releasing, and instantly, his eyes popped open and his gaze dropped to her lips, the urge to kiss her so great it hurt.

Instead, he let his eyes flick back up to meet hers and held as he chewed slowly. He took a step toward her, invading her space, his chest pressing against hers.

"What do you taste?" she asked.

"Cinnamon." He took her hand, ran his thumb over the finger he'd licked moments before. "Sugar." He eased her toward him. "And something else. Something I know by heart, yet I can't quite make sense of." He drew a slow breath, let the moment hold. "This is the one."

You're the one, he thought, the words on the tip of tongue, right there, eager to be spoken. But instead of saying them, he took a step back, breaking the hold and taking a breath.

So much for treading lightly…

Chapter 8

"Just go home," Kylie said to herself. She'd stopped at a traffic light, and turning one way would take her on to Franny's house. Which was the safe choice—the right choice.

But turning left…

She put on her right-hand turn signal and nodded to herself. "Good choice."

And then the light turned from red to green, and Kylie spun her wheel left instead.

"All right, so what are you going to say when you get there, huh?" she asked herself. "Hi, I don't know why I'm here, but I couldn't stop thinking about you, so it seemed only fitting that I show up at your house unannounced. Again." She hung her head. "God, this shouldn't be this hard, right?"

Automatically, she took the next right, then turned left onto his street. The problem with his house was that you couldn't stalk it. There was no driving by and him thinking it was just a random car. Oh no. His driveway was longer than some roads, which all meant that if she made the decision to pull down the driveway, there was no going back.

Ugh, ugh, ugh.

"Okay, you just need an excuse." She glanced around in her car, at her phone, then rummaged around in her purse. There was absolutely no reason for her to be there, and people didn't drop by for coffee at eight o'clock at night.

Wait…coffee. Coffee!

A grin spread across Kylie's face, and she pressed the accelerator as she turned down Brady's driveway.

The lights were on inside, the occasional flash of a TV showing that he was awake and watching a game.

She parked her car and stepped out before she chickened out. Shaking out her hands, she walked up his sidewalk and onto his front porch. It took another second or two for her to draw up the courage to ring the doorbell, and another few seconds for Brady to open the door.

His eyebrows shot up at the sight of her, but he was smiling. Smiling was good, right? Goodness, she was nervous.

"Hey," he said. "Did I forget something at the shop or something?"

No, but that would have made her life so much easier.

"Actually, I wanted to return your coffee mug to you."

Brady's eyes dropped to her hands—her very empty hands. Oh my God, she didn't have the freaking mug! How did she not realize that before ringing his doorbell?

A grin played at his lips. "Did you change your mind on the way here or something? Or are you hiding it somewhere?"

"Actually, I realized that I forgot it, but I was already here, so I thought I would say hi." She waved her hand awkwardly at him. "Hi."

He bit his lip in a clear effort to keep from laughing. "Hi."

Cringing, Kylie took a step back. *Retreat slowly, save your pride!* "All right then, I'll see you tomorrow." She turned around, sure her cheeks were redder than a jolly Santa's when Brady called out to her.

"Hey, I just made some dinner, which I hate doing, because I always end up with a ton of leftovers. Would you like to..." He motioned inside.

"I don't want to disturb your dinner."

"Honestly, you'd be doing me a favor," Brady said. "Plus, I'm a fantastic cook." He grinned at her, and she couldn't keep from grinning back.

"Sounds a little on the confident side."

He shrugged. "Why don't you come join me and decide for yourself?"

"If you're sure."

"One hundred percent. Join me."

Kylie stepped inside to the smell of peppers and onions cooking and a sizzling sound in the air. "Fajitas?"

"Chicken. I hope that's okay."

"It's perfect. What can I do to help?"

They made their way into the kitchen, and Brady stirred the chicken and vegetables, sautéing them with some sauce that smelled delicious. "You can throw together some guacamole real quick. I picked up some avocados at the store." Brady passed over two avocados and nodded toward his knife set. "Use whatever you want."

Nervousness swarmed through Kylie's stomach. Not only was Kylie a bad cook, but she was so bad that she made bad cooks look good. "Um, I've never made guacamole before."

"No problem. Just cut the avocado, scoop out the flesh, mash it, and mix in one-quarter cup from that jar of salsa on the island." He pointed to the jar.

"Right. I can do that." Kylie pulled a knife from the block by the oven and rested the avocados on the cutting board Brady had set out on the island beside the salsa. She sliced the fruit in half, removed the seed, then scooped out the flesh. Thank God she enjoyed watching Food Network or she would have had no idea how to slice the avocado.

"You look nervous," Brady said, passing over a mixing bowl and spatulas to mash and mix the dip.

"You think? I'm the worst cook on the planet, and if the smell is any indication, you're the next Bobby Flay."

He laughed. "Nah, you know my mom. She would never have let us leave her house without some basic understanding of cooking. I paid attention."

"I didn't know your mom taught you how to cook. I don't remember seeing it."

"She liked to do it when we were alone. It was her way of making sure she had individual time with each of us." Removing the fajitas from the hot stove eye, Brady took the avocado and mashed it in the mixing bowl, then scooped out several spoonfuls of salsa, dropped them in with the avocado, and mixed it all together.

"Your mom never cooked with you?" Brady asked, but Kylie could tell he wanted to take the question back. "I'm sorry, that was stupid. Of course she didn't."

"No, it's okay. Surprisingly, she did cook with me once. Bake, actually. They were having some fundraiser at school, and all her friends were submitting baked goods with their daughters. She bought a box of cake mix and some frosting. I'll never forget her laughter when the mixer threw some of the cake batter at us. She had it on her cheek." Kylie stared out into the common area adjacent to the kitchen, lost in her thoughts.

Brady plated fajitas, soft taco shells, guacamole, and chips for each of them. "Can you grab a couple of wine glasses from up there?" He motioned to the cabinet beside the refrigerator, and Kylie pulled out two.

They sat down at the large table in the breakfast nook, and Brady poured each of them a glass of white wine.

"Do you ever see her now?"

Kylie took a bite of her fajitas and closed her eyes in satisfaction. "Wow, this is good."

"Mama Littleton recipe."

"I'll have to compliment her on it the next time I see her." She took another bite, stalling, but she could feel Brady watching her, waiting on her to answer. "No, I don't see her. Or even talk to her, or my dad. They live in Florida now and are members of some country club there. They're busy."

"Do they know you're back in Crestler's Key?"

Kylie took a sip of her wine and thought about it. "I don't know. Maybe if Franny told them. I believe she talks to my mom from time to time."

"But you don't?"

"You know how they are."

And he did. Their first date was because her parents had forgotten her birthday. Missed birthday turned into forgotten Christmas presents, and soon, they went out of town for the holidays and she stayed with Franny.

Franny was a better mom than her actual mom anyway.

"I'm sorry they suck so badly. No one should have to deal with parents like that."

Taking another bite of her food, Kylie attempted to brush it off. "It's no big deal. They are who they are. I have Franny." She took her last bite of fajitas, then scooped up the last of the guacamole on her plate with a broken chip. "*Gah*, that was so good. I'm going to have to ask you to cook for me more often."

Brady's eyes met hers. "Anytime, name the date. It's just me here. Gets lonely sometimes."

Wind picked up outside, causing some tree limbs to smack. Whatever game Brady had been watching was still playing in the family room.

"I bet. Charlie and Zac seem happy."

Brady nodded as he steepled his fingers together and stared out over them. "They are."

"And you like their wives?"

At that, Brady laughed. "It's more that I tolerate them. Or at least that's the case with Zac's wife, Sophie. She's very opinionated and in your face about things. I'm surprised she hasn't introduced herself to you yet."

"No, but I've heard talk around town that she's a little on the loud side."

"That's Sophie—loud and feisty. Lila, Charlie's wife, is much nicer."

"I'm guessing Sophie gives you her opinion all the time, and that's why you don't like her as much? You never liked hearing others' opinions about you."

Brady laughed again. "Something like that." He picked up their plates and started for the sink, when Kylie grabbed his arm.

"No way. You cooked. I'll do the dishes." She took the plates, but Brady didn't relent.

"You're a guest. My mom would have my head if I had you cleaning the dishes."

Kylie set the plates by the sink and turned on the water, allowing it to warm up. "Is your dishwasher empty?" she asked.

"Always."

Her eyes lifted. "Always? Who can keep that pace?"

"I'm the only one here. Kind of easy to keep my dishes clean."

The sadness in his voice made Kylie glance up, but he wasn't looking at her. "So, then, we'll rinse them and place them in the dishwasher. It can do the washing."

They fell into silence as each rinsed a plate, then Brady closed the dishwasher and leaned against the counter, his arms crossed as he studied her.

"I sense a question," Kylie asked.

"I was just curious why you're alone."

"Tonight? Franny wanted to go to bed early so—"

"No, I mean, why are you single? Why aren't you married with two point five kids, living in a house with a white fence around it and playing with your dog in the backyard?"

A chill moved through Kylie at his suggestion, and how very much she didn't want to answer it. Instead, she walked away, toward his family room. "You know I hate dogs. I love these shelves," she added, running her hand over the shelves built into the back wall. A stone fireplace split the center, making the wall all stained wood shelves and stone. It was beautiful, just like the rest of the house.

Brady walked up beside her. "Right, but—"

"Thank you for dinner," Kylie said, cutting him off. She couldn't have this conversation with him, especially not here, where she felt so exposed.

"Kylie."

"It was amazing, truly. Thank you. And I'm sorry I barged in on you."

He stared at her, clearly contemplating whether he wanted to let it go. Finally, he glanced away, and Kylie knew she was safe again. "Any time. I'll walk you out."

"It's okay," she said, desperate to separate from him before she confessed that she was alone because she couldn't be with him. "I can find my way."

He walked her to the door anyway, opened it up, and she forced a smile. "Thanks again." Rising on her toes, Kylie quickly kissed his cheek, then stepped outside. Cold night air enveloped her, and she wrapped her hands around herself to try to warm.

She didn't look back.

Chapter 9

Kylie tapped her fingernails against the counter at Signs and More, her patience growing thinner with each passing second. It was Thanksgiving Day, and she should be back at Franny's, helping her prepare their small Thanksgiving meal, but instead she was there in her PJs, all because she needed to pick up the wooden Santa sign she'd paid to be created and showcased outside beginning on Black Friday. The sign was supposed to be ready on Monday, but here they were on Thursday, the day before she needed it, and she still didn't have the dang thing.

Which was exactly how she'd ended up there. Living in a small town had its perks, and her feistiness had spiked the day before, when she saw that Mike had closed the shop for "the holidays." All before delivering her promised sign. Well, screw that! So she drove over to his house, had tea with his lovely wife, and lo and behold, she had a call from him that the sign would be ready this morning.

Now, she was there, waiting as Mike finished doing whatever he needed to do to the thing in the back. For as long as he was taking, she wondered if he was cutting down a tree and carving up the sign this very second.

"All righty, here you go," Mike said with a cross between a smile and a scowl. "Here's the sign you just had to have on Thanksgiving Day. You did know that it's Thanksgiving, didn't you? Or maybe because you're not married with kids, you didn't think that kind of thing mattered to others."

Kylie gritted her teeth together, but with her sign in hand now, there was no point in dishing out the details. Or defending her lack of husband or kids situation. Those things were fact, and while it hadn't really bothered her before, it did bother her now that she was back in Crestler's Key.

"Thank you," she said instead and passed over the thirty bucks Mike had quoted her. "Happy Thanksgiving to you." Then she pushed out of the store before he could insult her any further and slammed right into someone.

"Oh! Sorry, I was—" Her words cut short as she took in the person she'd nearly taken out.

Brady smirked. "As agile as ever," he said. "Where are you off to in such a hurry?"

She lifted the sign. "Just picking up my Santa sign for tomorrow, then heading back to help Franny finish up Thanksgiving. You?"

That was when she noticed that he was fidgeting with his keys. "Actually, just picking someone up." He nodded ahead to the floral shop, and out stepped Valerie Brock—Miss Crestler's Key, Miss Homecoming Queen, Miss Forever Wanted Brady. But in the weeks Kylie had spent in town, she hadn't seen Valerie with Brady even once, so surely they weren't...

"Right."

Valerie walked up to them and smiled at Kylie. "Hi there. I heard you were back in town."

Kylie nodded slowly. "I am. It's good to see you."

"You, too. Wow, it's cold." She slipped her arm through Brady's. "You ready to go?"

He stared at Kylie, and she contemplated disappearing into the sidewalk. Of course he'd moved on. How could she not know this would happen? But then, why hadn't Valerie been in the shop to see him? Or maybe she had and Kylie just hadn't noticed. No, no, she would have noticed. So maybe this was a new thing and...Kylie was officially spiraling into obsessive-thoughts mode. It didn't matter when or how or why. Brady was no longer hers. None of the rest mattered.

"Well, see y'all later," she said with a smile to Valerie, then forcing herself to look up at Brady. "Tell your mama I said hello."

"I will." They started off and she made time getting down the sidewalk and away from the humiliation of seeing her ex-boyfriend with the girl he really should have been with. Valerie was short skirts and makeup and pom-poms. Kylie was a T-shirt girl, and back then she wore her hair in a ponytail more often than not and lip gloss was her one and only makeup item. She supposed some things worked out as they were supposed to, and this was one of them.

Stepping off the sidewalk, she unlocked her car, when Brady called out, "Ky."

Her head snapped up. "Yeah?"

He looked as though he wanted to say something important, but instead he said, "Have a nice Thanksgiving."

"Thanks. You, too."

* * * *

"That took forever," Franny said as Kylie made her way into the kitchen ten minutes later, her heart so heavy that she wondered how she walked at all.

"Sorry, ran into some distractions."

Franny's eyes lifted from the mixer, where she was blending sweat potatoes for her sweet potato casserole, the best in the world.

"Mike give you grief?"

"Not Mike, though he was plenty angry to be out on Thanksgiving. Thanks for putting in the call to Trish, by the way. Worked like a charm."

Her eyes lit. "Wives have a way of getting their husbands to do things no one else can get them to do. Now, why does your face look sad?"

Shrugging, Kylie leaned the sign against the bookcase across from the island, where Franny stacked all her cookbooks, though the woman had never used one in her life.

A thousand different scents floated around the air, and Kylie remembered when Brady had come to their Thanksgiving dinner instead of his parents'. It was a huge deal, and his mama hadn't been happy in the least. Kylie was petrified she'd be angry with her, but Brady was always the kind of person that would do what he wanted to do and would hear nothing else on it. That had been the first year that her parents went skiing for the holiday…without her.

Thank God for Franny stepping in, and Brady didn't want it to be a party of two, so he showed, too. Before long, neighbors came over and they had a full house. But Kylie never forgot Brady sacrificing spending time with his family to make her feel like she had one of her own.

"All right, spill it before I ruin these potatoes staring at you."

"Fine, but it's not a big deal. I ran into Brady on the way out. With Valerie Brock."

At that, Franny started laughing. "Lord, that girl's' had her eye on him since birth."

"I know. And she's nice."

"She is," Franny agreed. "Not at all like that Paige Stills he dated for a minute there." She shuddered. "That was a horrible combination."

Kylie stopped mid-motion to the coffee maker. "He dated Paige?"

Her godmother gave her a sympathetic look. "It's been ten years, child. He had to try."

"Right. Of course he did." Kylie grabbed a coffee cup and filled it up, took a drink, but even her love of coffee couldn't help with the bitter thoughts she was having. He was hers, and now...

"But..." Franny set down the mixer and walked over to her. "He never looked at any of them the way he looks at you."

"You mean looked at me. Past tense."

"No. I mean looks. You should see him light up when you walk into the shop. That man's heart is so tied up in you he can't see straight. Now, I don't know what's going on with Valerie. It's Thanksgiving, so it could just be an innocent invite to dinner. We do that here in the South, unless you've forgotten. I haven't seen her around. But even if not, don't worry about Brady and where he wants to be. Worry about you."

Kylie set down her coffee cup. "I know."

"You need to ask yourself if you want to be with Brady. And maybe more importantly, if you're strong enough to stay. Through the thick and thin. Through the doubts and worries. Because they'll always be there. But you have to trust him and trust that love of his for you. If you can do that, then I think that boy is yours and always has been. If not..."

"Then let him go," Kylie said, finishing the thought. "I know that, too."

Franny stared at her. "You know I love you. As though you were my own, even. But you have to open up that heart of yours. Or I fear you'll be alone, and I don't want that for you."

Nodding, Kylie walked around the island. "I'm going to grab a shower, then I'll be back down to help you finish up."

"Sounds good. We'll be eating in an hour."

Kylie took her phone and went upstairs, started the shower, and prepared to allow the water to help her sort out her thoughts, when a text came through.

Brady: I'm not with Valerie.

Her heart sped up at the text, everything the text might mean swirling through her mind. Should she say good? Should she admit that she was relieved? Should she ask what she was doing with him then?

No, no, and more no.

Slowly, she picked up the phone, started texting, then deleted it, set it back down and paced around the bathroom. She picked it up again, texted and deleted. Then did it again. She set the phone down hard on the counter. "Ugh! I should just call him."

Siri spoke up. "Calling Brady Cell."

Her eyes widened. "No, no, no. No calling Brady's cell." Kylie went for the phone, but it slipped out of her grasp and hit the bathroom floor. She scrambled for it, only to pick it up and see that, in fact, Siri had called him.

"Hello? Ky?"

Crap, crap, crap.

"Um, hey. Sorry, Siri called you on accident."

"Siri called me." She could hear the humor in his voice.

"Exactly."

"Not you. Siri."

"That's what I said. You know that happens all the time."

The smile in his voice made her wish she was there with him instead of Valerie. "Of course it does. To you."

"Hey! Not just to me. You're telling me that's never happened to you?"

"Not once. But I have—wait, is that the shower running in the background?"

Kylie cringed. "Yes. I was about to get in the shower when you called."

"You mean when you called."

"No, when Siri called."

"Riiight."

She smiled. God it felt good to talk to him.

"Anyway, sorry Siri bothered you. You can get back to whatever you were doing." *Please don't let it be* who *you were doing.*

"Ky."

"It's okay, really."

"Is it? Really?" He waited, and Kylie contemplated whether to say what she felt or what she should feel. Which was what exactly? She was so confused.

"I just want you to be happy," she said finally. "That's all I ever wanted."

"Right," he said, and Kylie closed her eyes in anger at herself. Why couldn't she just tell him that no, it wasn't all right. None of this was all right. Because they were supposed to be together, he was supposed to be with her and only her. But she couldn't.

"Okay, well, enjoy your Thanksgiving. I better get back," she said.

"To your shower."

"Exactly."

"Quite an image you're leaving me with there," he said, turning playful, and Kylie released a slow breath. God, she loved him. That was the truth. She loved him, had never stopped, the feeling so intense it was difficult to even think it, but there it was and there it had always been.

"Bye, Brady," she said with a smile. "Will I see you tomorrow?"

"You will. Are you planning to hit up Target for the toy?"

"Later today. They open at five, so I'll be there with bells on."

"All right then. Be safe…and warm. See you tomorrow," he said, then the call ended and Kylie forced herself to set her phone back down.

It was time she had a heart-to-heart with herself and her fears. Brady may not be offering her anything right now, but he was taking a small step. Could she forgive their past enough to meet him halfway?

Chapter 10

Brady parked out back of Southern Dive at five a.m. on Black Friday, prepared to say a quick hello to his brother Charlie, who was manning the main shop, while he held down things at ETC.

He'd been out until one a.m. the night before, trying to find one of those robotic dolls for Ally's kid, all to come up empty.

Target was his first stop, then Walmart, then Kohl's and CVS, and he even went to Ace Hardware just to see, but all they did was look at him like he was insane. Which, clearly, he was.

A part of him wanted to call Kylie and ask if she'd had any luck, but then he didn't want to tell her that he was looking, too. Admitting that hinted at him caring about things he shouldn't care about, and threw serious doubt on the being-over-Kylie image he attempted to present to anyone who would half listen.

He hadn't even intended to search for the toy. It was all an accident, after his sister, Kate, asked if he needed her to look for anything while she was out shopping. At first, he'd immediately said no, then it occurred to him that he did have something in mind, and the rest was six-hour-long shopping spree history.

To be honest, he wasn't sure what he would do if he found the doll. Wrap it and do the anonymous thing? Tell Kylie that he found it, then deal with the question of why he was looking? And then he'd be forced to reveal the truth: that he wanted to see her face light up when he delivered. That for him, everything always circled back to her.

But then that was stupid, and it didn't matter anyway—he couldn't find the damn thing.

"Lifesaver," Charlie said, as Brady passed over the cup of coffee he'd brought him.

"Heard you got roped into shopping with Kate. You know how she is, if you stay too long after dinner, you'll always end up being her shopping partner. Nobody wants any part of that. Why you think Alex always drives separately?"

Brady laughed. "Yeah, well, had a little shopping of my own this year, so thought I might as well help her while I was at it."

The truth was it had been fun, and it had been a long time since he'd spent any alone time with his sister. Of course, he used the time to feel out her thoughts on Kylie, because though Charlie was the shrink of the family, Kate was always the most direct. If she said he should walk, then he should. Whether he did it or not was another thing altogether.

But Kate hadn't told him to walk. Or at least, she hadn't told him to walk away. She told him to take it slow, and then, if he was sure, one-hundred-percent sure, that Kylie was the one, to lay it all on the line and hope for the best.

"You tired or distracted?" Charlie said.

"Little of both."

"Kylie?"

Brady hesitated. He'd never been one to hold back his thoughts on anything, but at the same time, he didn't want to hear all the reasons he was sure to get screwed. Kylie had trust issues and security issues and probably other issues that all meant she would never truly open up and might always feel the need to pull away.

But there had been a time when she believed him when he said he loved her more than life itself, that she would always come first, and that he would never leave her.

And then he did.

Though he hadn't ended their relationship, looking back on it, he could see why his decision to go to college halfway across the country could read as abandonment. For him, it was just another adventure, another opportunity for them to go somewhere together. He assumed she would want to go, too. But he'd been foolish and selfish and every other word to describe a seventeen-year-old who thought of himself above everyone else. Worse, he thought they'd do the long distance thing, but he never considered that she would shut down, that she would walk away and never look back.

"You don't have to talk about her if you don't want to," Charlie said finally. "But I'm here if you need anything, and if I can say one thing?"

Brady glanced over at his brother. "Of course."

"I know firsthand how badly it sucks to love someone and feel like you can't be with her. If you love her, if you want her…then do whatever you got to do. Trust yourself to know what's best for you and what you can take. And then trust yourself enough to know when to walk away if that's the right thing to do."

Nodding slowly now, Brady looked at the ground.

"Right."

"I'm not trying to go the negative route, 'cause I think this could work for you two this time. You're both back in town, you're both more settled. It's a good time to see what could happen. I just don't want you to go dark like you did last time."

Brady nodded again, unable to say anything. He hadn't realized at the time how much he'd withdrawn from the family after Kylie left. He thought he had covered up his feelings. Apparently, he was delusional.

"Just looking out for you, little brother. You know you're my favorite."

This time Brady smiled, because he did know this, but Charlie rarely said it. "Likewise, man. I appreciate it, truly. But I'm okay. I've got this under control."

He hoped.

"All right, gotta head over there and get things started up. Give me a yell if you need extra hands on this side."

Charlie waved him on. "I've got this. See ya later."

They said good-bye, and Brady made his way to Merrily Christmas. The small sign for Southern Dive & ETC stood just outside the door, but today, the wooden SANTA IS HERE! sign had been propped up against it, hiding the company name from view. A few weeks ago, this would have started a fight, but today, instead of arguing, Brady found himself adjusting the Santa sign for better view by people passing by.

He smiled a little at the tiny reindeer cut into the wood and how angry Mike must have been to be asked to do it. His gaze drifted up to look inside the windows, and that was when he zeroed in on Kylie, pacing in front of Ally, her hands tossing in the air and then covering her face before repeating the sequence all over again.

"What, did Santa not show?" he asked from the door. She turned to look at him, her eyes wide in panic. "Shit. Your Santa didn't show."

Her hands flew into the air again. "He didn't show! What kind of Santa doesn't show? I booked him ages ago and I called and there's no one else. Every other Santa with the service is booked and I've been advertising this thing in the paper for weeks and I had Mike make that sign and Annie-Jean has been giving out flyers at the bakery and everyone knows. And oh my God, the kids. The kids are going to come here expecting to see Santa and give their lists and be happy, but instead, they're going to be told there is no Santa today. Which, you know, will just make them wonder if there really is no Santa at all, because Santa would surely show, but he's not here, so that must mean—"

Brady was to her in three long steps. He placed his hands on her small shoulders and bent down so they were eye to eye. "Breathe. This isn't death. We'll figure something out."

"It kind of is, though. Santa's death. At least in our store."

"Girl, you did not just say Santa's death," Ally said coming around. "And anyway, I've got an idea."

Kylie glanced over at her as though all the hope in the world rested on her idea. Ally took a step back, and Brady fought the urge to laugh. It was a lot of pressure to see that hope in Kylie's eyes and know you were the sole one to help keep it there. "Well, go on."

"All right, but you're scaring me a bit. Maybe breathe, like Mr. Hottie here said."

Brady grinned. "I could get used to that name."

Waving a hand at him to hush, Ally continued. "I have a Santa costume at home. My husband dressed up one year at his office, and we forgot to return the thing. Anyway, I can go get it."

"But then what? Who can play Santa?"

Ally's grinned turned to Brady and it was his turn to take a step back. "No way. No freaking way will you get me into a Santa getup."

"But you have to. We don't have anyone else. It's Black Friday. People are going to be here any second, and the Santa visit starts in an hour. I'll cover your side of the shop while Franny covers ours and Kylie manages your crowd. We can do this if you help. You don't want to be responsible for kids crying on Christmas, now do you?"

He deadpanned. "It's not Christmas."

"Same difference."

Brady ran his hands over his face and forced himself to look over at Kylie, but he already knew what he would find there. She was watching him, chewing her thumbnail, the word *please* written across her face. "I can't believe I'm going to do this."

"You'll do it?" She grabbed his hands and started jumping up and down, and any debate about it was over. Damn, why couldn't he tell this woman no?

"You are going to owe me big for this. Like a year's worth of owing. I'm starting my list today."

She nodded along. "Absolutely. Whatever you want, I'll do it. Name it and it's yours. Just please help me here. Please."

* * * *

Kylie stared at the man who captured her heart that night in an art studio, when her parents both forgot her birthday and she was feeling like a ghost of a person. He smiled to cheer her up and then insisted they go out, and little did he know, he saved her that day. She laughed for the first time in a long time, and suddenly her aching heart had a new reason to ache—this time for a boy.

A jock, of all types of boys.

A boy so far out of her league she was surprised he was even talking to her.

And yet, he seemed just as taken by her.

It took no time for her to say she loved him. She said it first, because she couldn't for the life of her keep it inside any more. It took him longer, and for a beat, she worried that he was pulling back, when he bought her a small heart necklace, gave it to her, and said the words she had longed to hear.

"What do you say, Brady? Save me one more time, for old time's sake?"

A slow smile curved his lips and his eyes cut over to Ally. "Fine, go get it, but y'all can forget me saying 'ho, ho, ho.'"

The women laughed and Ally went in to hug him while Kylie watched, her eyes connected with his as she mouthed thank you.

"Just add it to the list."

She scoffed. "List?"

Ally ran out the door to go to her house and grab the Santa costume, and Brady made his way over to his side of the shop, Kylie following behind. She knew even before he turned that he was grinning in that almost laughing way.

"What list?"

He crossed his arms and leaned his hip against his counter. "You know, the list of all the times I've bailed you out and all the ways I feel you should make it up to me."

"Wait a second. You've decided how I should say thanks? What kind of nonsense is that? I'll make this up to you."

"Oh, yeah? How?" He started for her, each step making it harder and harder for her to breathe.

Kylie tucked her hair behind her ears and prayed it wasn't obvious that her heart was beating out of control. "What do you want?"

He stopped inches from her and peered down. "I have a few things in mind."

"Like."

"Like..." Brady dropped his head toward hers, his eyes darting up to check for permission, when Franny came bustling in from the back.

"I swear to God people are insane. I tried to do a little shopping this morning, trying to pick up a gift for Ally's daughter Rena, and was ran over by a shopping cart. You should have seen these—" Franny stopped short, like she was just seeing them for the first time. A bright smile split her face. "I'm sorry. Didn't realize I was interrupting something."

Kylie took a deliberate step back, her focus on anything but Brady, and she wanted to scream at herself. Even though she'd only made that one move, she was running again. She could feel it. "You weren't interrupting anything."

"Right. You weren't," Brady said, his tone clear. He was disappointed in her, but his disappointment was nothing compared to her own. Why couldn't she take a leap of faith? Why couldn't she just for once be a normal person without all these fears clouding her judgment? This wasn't seventeen-year-old Brady with life aspirations so much larger than her own. He lived here now, like her. He bought a house. He wasn't leaving.

So why couldn't she trust him to stay?

"I'm just going to go get the coffee and hot chocolate stand set up," she said, making a beeline for the back and bumping into a display of wooden angels on the way. The display swayed and Kylie steadied it. "That was almost a disaster," she said with an awkward laugh, while Brady and Franny continued to stare at her with blank expressions. "Right, so the coffee. I'm just going to..." She motioned to the back and slipped through the door before she messed up anything else.

She stopped in front of the Keurig and hung her head. "Fantastic. Seriously. You are a rock star."

"Um, are you talking to the coffee maker, or to me? Because yes I am."

Kylie turned around to find Ally closing the back door, Santa suit in hand, and immediately her spirits lifted. "You. One hundred percent you! I owe you huge for this."

"Girl, whatever. We're a little team here at Merrily. Everyone has to help. I'm glad this time it was me to be able to fill the job."

"And now I have to hug you." Kylie walked over and draped an arm around the woman, squeezed, then released and focused back on the coffee. She removed the water reservoir from the coffee maker, walked over to the sink, and filled it up with water, then she replaced it and bent down to search for k-cups in the box she kept below the coffee maker on the shelf. "Do you mind giving it to Brady?"

Without having to look her way, Kylie knew what she would find on Ally's face—a question mark. A giant question mark, and at this point, she had one in her own mind, too. Despite everything, she found herself pulling back, that age-old fear that someone else was going to not show, disappoint her—leave—was there, ready to dampen her spirit.

"No."

At that, Kylie glanced up. "Sorry?"

"I'm sorry, but I said no. You need to give it to him. He's your friend."

Sighing, Kylie pulled out a dozen k-cups, eight caffeinated and four decaffeinated. Then she opened the box beside it labeled TEA, pulled out four, and did the same with the box beside that, labeled HOT CHOCOLATE. Finally, she stood up and turned to face Ally, who was quickly becoming her only friend in the town. "He's not my friend."

"Okay, lover. Whatever."

And now she couldn't help rolling her eyes.

"Still counts if you wish he was your lover, and obviously you do, because you are a living, breathing woman and he looks like David Beckham."

"I do?" a deep voice called from across the room. "I always thought I looked more like Theo James. Plus, Beckham's got all those tattoos, right?"

Kylie swallowed and forced herself to look over at him, curious if he'd heard her say that they weren't friends. Their eyes met, his so full of emotion she wanted to cry. Clearly, he'd heard, and clearly she sucked, but they weren't friends. It had been a long, long time since she considered Brady a friend. That part wasn't untrue.

"Well, since there's enough awkward tension in this room to slice through ice, I'm going to just go up front. I can take the coffee for you, Ky," Ally said, dropping the Santa suit onto the table beside her and reaching out for the coffee maker.

She tried to flash a smile, to make light of the whole thing, but instead it came out as a grimace. "Thanks."

Ally disappeared through the swinging door into the front of the store, leaving her alone with Brady, and there was no going another moment without her saying what was on her mind. That was thing about her: it was easy to unveil her thoughts and feelings. Trusting others? Another story altogether.

The space was quiet, and with only one light on it was easy to say what she should have said the first time she saw him again. "I'm sorry," she whispered, unable to say them louder. "For a lot of things. But most of all, I'm sorry for what I just said and for you hearing it. Because I think despite everything we've been through, maybe you were the only true friend I ever had, and it's crappy to suggest otherwise. We may not be friends now, but we were. Great friends. So, I'm sorry."

Brady cocked his head, and she thought he was about to let her have it. For leaving all those years ago, for being the one to walk away, for being a true jerk to him since the first time she saw him here. But instead of saying any of those things, he released a breath, and then diverted his eyes to the Santa suit on the table. "Is that my getup for the morning?"

Running her hand over the Santa suit, Kylie pictured Brady wearing it and couldn't help but laugh. "This is you, if you're still willing to help."

He stared at her for a long time, and Kylie thought he was backing out. Maybe she could fit into the costume if she stuffed it with some of the holiday throw pillows they sold in Merrily. "Look, I understand this is asking a lot, so I get it if you want to—"

"I do what I say, Ky. Always. But I do have one question."

"Yes?"

A crooked smile curved his lips. "Where's your elf suit? 'Cause I'm not suffering alone!"

A relieved laugh broke free, which quickly turned into fits when he slipped on the beard.

"Get going, little elf. Someone has to keep it organized. I'd say that someone is you."

Kylie glanced around the stockroom, her eyes landing on a mix of Santa and elf hats for the hat decorating she'd planned for the following week. With the fitted red turtleneck and jeans she'd put on that morning, she could pull off being an elf.

"All right, Santa. You have yourself an elf."

Chapter 11

"Ho, ho, ho. *Ho, ho, ho!*" Brady stared at his reflection in the bathroom mirror. His tanned skin contrasted sharply with the white, cottony mustache and beard and the long white wig left no question that it was fake, but he could do the ho, ho, ho thing as good as anyone.

A soft knock came from the other side of the door. "You ready, Santa?"

He opened the door to find Kylie dressed in the elf hat and elf shoes she'd pulled from one of her weekly craft shops. She'd put on red lipstick and extra blush, then some shimmer stuff on her eyes. She looked beautiful.

"Confession?" he asked.

Kylie glanced down at her outfit, then back at him with a grimace. "Yeah?"

He leaned into her and whispered, "Santa is having very naughty thoughts about his elf right now."

A laugh broke from her lips and as he peered down at her, that bright smile on her face, it took everything in him not to kiss her.

"You two coming?" Ally called from the swinging door. "These kids are getting restless."

Kylie took a step back, and Brady wished he could reach out to stop her, force her to stay instead of always leaving. "I'll go out and announce you. Then you come through the door. We have everything set up out there for you."

With a nod that he understood, she turned away. Once she cleared the door, Ally started for him. "Be patient with her. She's scared. Don't confuse her fear with disinterest, 'cause that girl wants you. Badly. I can see it all over her face. Just be patient."

"I'm trying."

Ally planted her hands on her hips. "Try harder, Santa. It's Christmas. Let the magic do its job." Then she followed after Kylie.

Drawing a breath, Brady let Ally's words soak in. He had always been the kind of person who operated at a faster speed than everyone else. He did, while others planned. He reached the answer, while others were figuring out the problem. And that fast-thinking attitude had cost him Kylie once. Ally was right—he would have to learn patience if he hoped to win her trust again.

"Are you ready to see Santa?" Kylie's voice carried through the door, followed by cheers. A lot of cheers. The shop must be packed out. "Here he is!"

Brady pushed through the swinging door and immediately sounded off with his perfected, "*Ho, ho, ho!*" The kids all went crazy.

"This way, Santa," Kylie said, her eyes sparkling with happiness, and he couldn't help but smile back.

The store was more crowded than he'd ever seen it, with a line winding around inside, and then outside and along the sidewalk. Franny and Ally passed out hot chocolate, coffee, and warm cookies. Everyone, every single person, wore a grin of excitement. Now this was Christmas.

Brady took his seat at a throne-like chair with holiday decor all around it. A Christmas tree sat to his right, an elaborate Polar Express train set ran around and around its track to his left. The photos would be amazing. Kylie had outdone herself.

"Santa, this is Tanner," Kylie said, helping the first kid in line onto his knee. A small, blond boy with giant blue eyes peered up at him in awe. The older kids might not buy that he was Santa, but the little ones seemed to.

"Have you been good this year, Tanner?"

The little boy nodded so hard it was a wonder he didn't pull a muscle in his neck. Brady laughed.

"That's wonderful. What would you like for Christmas this year?"

The boy immediately eyed his mom, who was waiting beside the photographer Kylie had hired for the event. Though, photographer might be a stretch, since this was Zac's daughter, Carrie-Anne, and Kylie was paying her a hundred dollars to take the pictures. Honestly, she probably would have taken them for free.

"My mom wants me to say that I want a basketball goal."

"That sounds nice. All right, basketball goal it—"

"But what I really want," the boy said, his voice dropping to a whisper, "is a Barbie Jeep. The pink one. My friend, Zoey, has the Frozen Jeep, and it's blue, but I like pink better. Don't you like pink better?"

The mom approached then, clear embarrassment on her face. "I'm so sorry. Tanner, your time is up."

"But I need Santa to hear about the Jeep. How else will he know which one?"

"Tanner Matthew, we have talked about this."

Kylie stepped in then and bent down to Tanner's level. "Actually, when I was little I always wanted the Barbie car. They didn't have a Jeep back then, but I've seen the Jeep. It's pink and has a real radio, right?"

The boy's face lit up. "That's the one!"

"Well, I will make sure Santa knows which one to bring you."

Immediately, the boy's eyes went back to his mom. "But what if Mommy doesn't want me to have it?"

Kylie stood then and squared off with the mom. "Santa will respect your mom's wishes. But I'm sure your mom wouldn't put something as silly as gender stereotypes ahead of your happiness at Christmas. Would you?"

The mom's gaze fell to her son and clear guilt crossed her face. "No, of course not. Ask…ask for whatever you want."

"Really?" Tanner asked, then he launched into his mom's arms before turning back on Brady until he was inches from Brady's face. "I'll take a pink Barbie Jeep, please."

Brady's grin spread. "One Barbie Jeep, got it."

The family walked away holding hands, and Brady shook his head in respect at Kylie. "Still standing up for the little guys, I see."

She stood proud. "Everyone's a little guy to someone. Might as well stand up for the ones I can. Wouldn't you do the same?"

"You're unbelievable, do you know that?"

Her face lit up as her eyes trailed over him from head to toe. "You're pretty great yourself, Santa." Then she focused back on the crowd, which seemed to be doubling by the second. She grimaced. "Though, you might hate me after today."

Hate? His thoughts were leaning toward a completely different word. A word that scared the shit out of him, but he was in too deep now. There was no going back.

Chapter 12

"Coffee, sweet coffee," Kylie said as she made her way into the kitchen and reached for the full pot.

She and Brady stayed late at the stop, long after the Santa photos ended and the crowd died down. They both claimed that they needed to clean up, make sure their sides of the shop were ready for Saturday's business, and on and on with the excuses. But the truth was, she wanted to be near him. Something had changed that day; Brady dressed in Santa gear, her greeting family after family. It almost felt like maybe, just maybe, she wasn't alone anymore.

Pouring herself a cup of coffee, she was thankful that Franny woke early. There was always coffee waiting. Though, Kylie thought, she should wake crazy early once in a while to make it for Franny. That would require a five a.m. wake up. Maybe even four.

"Hey, Franny, what time do you wake up?" Kylie asked after pouring herself a cup. But no one answered. She walked into the family room to find the news on, yet there was no sign of her godmother. That was odd. Maybe she went into her room to grab something.

Kylie eyed the news, the talk of politics that never sat well with Franny or herself, for that matter.

"Fran, you in there?" she asked as she peeked inside her room, the master bedroom of the house. Simple, Southern charm dotted every wall and corner. An ivory quilt with pale roses covered her bed. "Franny?"

And that when she heard the water running in the bathroom. Franny never left water running, not even when she brushed her teeth. It was something about her great-grandmother having a well and instilling in her a deep-seated belief in water conservation. But now, the clear sound of water rushing from a faucet hit Kylie's ears, and she knew even before her legs started moving that something was wrong.

Prayers hit in her head one after the other, everything slowing down even though she was running. She rushed through the room and came to a halt at the doorway to the master bath, and suddenly all the blood drained from her head as her heartbeat sped up and her breathing became labored. "Franny!"

Kylie crumbled on the ground beside her godmother, her only family, clear panic on Franny's face. She was breathing, which was the only thing keeping Kylie together, but her face was pale, and she was clenching her chest. "Heart. Heart," she said.

"I'm here. It's all going to be okay."

Adrenaline kicked in, and Kylie ran from the room, grabbed the cordless phone beside Franny's phone and dialed 911 before dropping back beside her godmother. Tears streamed down her face, despite her ordering herself to calm down. Everything would be okay. This was Franny, the toughest person she knew. And yet, as she stared down at her, she looked frail.

Placing a hand on her face, she assured her over and over that everything would be okay, and then she gave the 911 operator their address and closed her eyes.

God, save her. Please...save her.

* * * *

Kylie paced back and forth at the foot of Franny's hospital bed, her hands wringing, her eyes still bloodshot from tears that had long since dried, only to be replaced with the type of fear that comes from realization.

Franny wouldn't be with her for much longer.

Thankfully, the amazing doctors and nurses at Crestler's Key Memorial worked miracles through the night to stabilize Franny, but in the end, Kylie learned that Franny had kept a big secret from her—she had heart disease, and had for some years. Her doctor had placed her on a strict diet and exercise regimen. Which, of course, Franny had never abided by.

This time, she was lucky—her heart attack, while scary, was minor, but the next time? She might not survive.

The thought was too much to take.

"Kylie, please let me get you some coffee." Kylie glanced over to Franny's nurse, Lauren, who was twenty-eight and newly engaged and wanted three children and a brick house over on Summer Street. Her fiancé was a UPS delivery guy, and they met because the hospital was one of the deliveries on his route.

It was one of many stories Kylie had learned through the night. She had asked every question she could ask of every doctor, nurse, or technician willing to talk to her, all in an effort to avoid the fearful thoughts that refused to go away.

"I'm okay."

"You haven't slept or eaten since you arrived. Please let me grab you a cup of coffee."

"I brought her one."

Kylie's eyes darted to the doorway, her heart picking up speed, all the emotions she'd bottled up in her stomach rushing to the surface. Tears pricked her eyes for the thousandth time in so many hours as she took in Brady's form, an overnight bag in one hand, a cup of coffee in the other.

"What are you doing here?"

"Becca Hamilton was working the night shift when Franny was brought in. She called Nick, who called Alex, who told Kate, who then called me."

Goodness, this community really was one giant family. "That's…" Her bottom lip trembled, and Brady nodded to Lauren and then set down the coffee and bag and pulled Kylie into his arms. His spicy, clean scent hit her, comforting her, as his arms became the security blanket she needed. How had she ever let him go?

"How is she?"

"Stable. They're saying it was minor, but she has some blockage, and if she doesn't make changes to her diet and lifestyle, then she could have another episode—perhaps a worse one—and she might not survive that time."

Brady's body tensed against her before he corrected and said, "No way. This is Franny. She's tougher than Superman."

Despite everything, Kylie smiled against his shoulder. "I'm going to tell her you said that. You know, when she wakes up." She pulled back then, but Brady grabbed her hand before she could fully separate.

"She's going to be fine."

The hospital had grown quiet some hours before, the rustle from earlier settling into the occasional footsteps, beeps from another room, or hushed voices. It had to be four a.m. now, and Kylie thought she might fall over from exhaustion.

A yawn rounded her mouth, despite her effort to fight it, and Brady's eyebrows pulled together. "Has she woken up at all?"

Kylie's gaze drifted over to her godmother. She looked like a ghost of the person she had always known. "She's stirred a bit, but they're keeping her stable with medicine that has her pretty knocked out. The doctor said she would wake and would be okay, but if you'd seen her. She…" A shaky hand went to her mouth like it could somehow stop the emotions from coming, and Brady gripped her hand tighter.

"Did he seem legit?"

"Who?"

"The doctor."

A smile split her face for the second time. God, Brady could cure the greatest of sadnesses. "*She* is wonderful."

Brady grinned back. "Liked that, didn't you?"

"More than you know." She yawned again, and Brady motioned to the small reclining chair behind her.

"Why don't you try to get some rest? The nurses will wake you if something happens, and you'll be right here if—when—Franny wakes. You're not helping her by hurting yourself."

Kylie wanted to sleep, but she was wired, every inch of her tensed with nervousness. "I don't know if I could. I'm worried, and I've never been able to sleep when I'm worried."

"I know," Brady said. "Remember when you were waiting to see if you'd been accepted to UK? I don't know if you slept a week for months."

She nodded and forced another smile, but this one didn't feel as relieving as the others. What if Franny didn't wake? What if she only had moments left with her? How could she spend those sleeping, when she should be taking in every detail, remembering every memory? "That was different."

"It was. But it doesn't change the fact that she would want you to rest, and you'll be more help to her when she wakes if you sleep for a bit. I'll stay to watch her and let you know if something happens, okay?" He led her over to the chair and eased her down. She was a zombie, dead on her feet, so she did little to fight it.

"You'll stay?"

"The whole time."

Kylie yawned again and leaned back in the chair. "Just for a few minutes." Her eyes closed before she'd consciously decided to close them, and she felt warm breath against her temple, then a swift kiss to her forehead, before she drifted off to sleep.

Chapter 13

"How did you get her to sleep?"

Brady glanced over to find that the nurse who had been in the room when he first came had returned, a clipboard in her hand. He pushed off the wall, where he'd been leaning for the better part of an hour, because when he sat down, he couldn't see Kylie. She kept mumbling in her sleep, her face tensing before relaxing again, and he feared she was having a nightmare.

When they were teenagers, she used to get them a lot, and he would smooth a hand over her hair until she relaxed and fell back to sleep. Now, he did the same, but with each touch, he found himself falling deeper and deeper into her trance.

"I helped her into the chair, exhaustion seemed to do the rest."

The nurse grinned, then walked over and checked on Franny, then jotted some things on her clipboard. "Kylie didn't tell me she had a boyfriend."

"She doesn't, or—I'm not. Just a friend."

Her right eyebrow lifted. "Who's by her side in the middle of a Friday night after Thanksgiving? I call that a boyfriend, but feel free to call yourself whatever you like."

He didn't argue with her, partially because he liked the sound of the word. "How is she?" he asked, nodding toward Franny.

"Stable. And lucky. But she will be okay."

Releasing a breath, he leaned back against the wall, just as Kylie's phone pinged once, then twice, then vibrated. He peered over, at first certain he shouldn't look, but then he caught what was on the screen. It wasn't a text. It was a notification.

REAL N FEEL IN STOCK, WALMART, BROWN HAIR GIRL DOLL

The toy was in stock at Walmart!

Brady quickly took out his own phone, opened Safari, and opened the Walmart app. He typed in the toy's name, and options populated the screen, but as he scanned down the list, he realized every one of them was out of stock. Dang, that lasted all of five seconds before the toy was snatched up and the stock depleted again.

"Man." He quickly ran a search on Toys "R" Us, and then Target, with the same results as Walmart, all out of stock, but then he remembered that Kylie said Target received a few each day.

Which meant they would receive a few *today*.

Checking the time, Brady felt a new sense of purpose. He couldn't fix Franny, he couldn't guarantee that she would be okay, and he couldn't take away that pain. But he could go stand in line at four thirty in the morning at a Target that wouldn't open until eight in an effort to fulfill Rena's Christmas wish, and in turn, Kylie's.

He bent down and kissed Kylie's forehead again, then slipped from the room. The hospital hallway was quiet, the nurse's station empty except for Franny's nurse, who was bent over her phone, a smile on her face.

"Hey, sorry to interrupt you," he said as he approached.

She glanced up, the smile still in place. "No, sorry. Just a text from my fiancé. Anyway, what can I do for you?"

"A text caused that big of a grin?"

The nurse shrugged. "Hasn't anyone ever made you so happy that little things make your day? Even a simple hello?"

Brady swallowed. He could think of someone.

"Right. Well, I need to be somewhere and will be gone for a few hours. Can you let Kylie know that I'll be back if she wakes? I'd text her, but I'm afraid it would wake her up."

"Of course," she said, then she took Brady's number, and he headed for the elevator.

* * * *

Kylie woke with a start, her heart racing, her cheeks wet from tears she hadn't remembered shedding. She blinked once, then twice, and her focus adjusted from sleep.

The heart attack.

The hotel room.

That was all part of the dream, too, but her dream ended at a gravesite, Franny's name etched into the gravestone.

Needing more proof, Kylie pushed to standing and laid a hand over Franny's heart, felt the beating, and watched the rise and fall of her chest. She was alive...for now.

The thought was enough to cause her own heartbeat to pick up speed again, her thoughts racing in search of a way to fix this, but there was nothing she could do. Nothing!

She hung her head and tried to remember that this wasn't Franny's last day. This was a bad day, a horrible, horrible day. But it wouldn't be her last day...horrible or otherwise.

Life was full of good and bad days, some so hopeless you wondered how you would go on. Kylie knew—she'd had a few of those herself. And that was when she remembered that Brady had been there when she went to sleep. But where was he now?

Turning back for the chair, she picked up her phone, hoping to find a text from Brady to let her know where he'd gone, something, but instead she found a notification that the Target closest to Crestler's Key had received a few Real N Feel dolls.

Her chest heaved as she took in each word. Franny was sick and there was nothing she could do to change that. Brady broke his promise and left her—again—and there was nothing she could do to change that. But damn if she was going to give up on finding Rena's doll.

Quickly, Kylie grabbed her coat and rushed from the room, pocketing her phone in the effort.

"Hi there," she said to the new nurse at the station. "My name is Kylie, and I'm Franny Waters's goddaughter. She's in room 245." Kylie pointed to the room.

"Yes, dear. I'm Sue, and Lauren filled me in about your godmother. Is there something I can do for you?"

Kylie drew a breath. She didn't want to leave, but she needed to do this. Her sanity was a thin string, ready to snap. She needed to do something to prove that life still held promise and hope. "I need to grab something really quick. Can you please call me if anything goes wrong? Anything at all?"

"Of course. It's just after seven. Your godmother may sleep for a bit longer. But I will call you if she wakes."

Kylie glanced back at the room, when the nurse placed her hand on Kylie's. "It's okay. She's in very good hands. Go do what you need to do. For you."

Nodding, Kylie fought back her emotions. "You'll call me?"

"I will call you. Promise."

And that did it. "But see, someone else already made me a promise today, and he broke it. And Franny is here, and what if she wakes and I'm not here, and then she—she—" She sucked in a breath, and the nurse stood and took Kylie's other hand.

"She will be okay. You will be okay. But it sounds like you could use a breath. It isn't selfish to take care of yourself. You matter here, too."

The halls were busier now, nurses doing their rounds, doctors popping into rooms. It reminded Kylie that Franny had survived the night. Day was breaking outside.

"Go. I will call you. And I never break my promises." She winked, and Kylie said a quick thank you before rushing to the elevator.

Christmas music hit her ears once inside, and she tried to remember that this season wasn't about worry or fear. It was about miracles and love and a general feeling that something greater existed in this world than just ourselves.

The doors pinged open and Kylie ran for it, bursting from the main doors and running with all she had to her car. It wasn't until she turned the ignition that she realized the time—seven thirty.

Seven thirty, no. Target opened at eight, and Kylie was easily twenty minutes away. The line would be around the building. Heck, by that point, it would probably be circling the building over and over again.

Doubt and hopelessness crept up, but then she glanced up and caught a young boy helping an older man to the main door of the hospital. She watched the boy, assuming maybe he was a grandson or relative of some kind, but then the boy ran off to his mother's waiting hand, and they walked hand-in-hand to her car.

A stranger. The elderly man was a stranger whom the boy chose to help out of kindness.

Kylie wouldn't give up on this. Not today or tomorrow. Rena was getting this toy. Besides, it was the Sunday after Black Friday now, which meant church. There was a slight chance that few would show up at Target so early when they needed to be at church later.

The idea made her feel better, and she cranked up the Christmas music as she sped down the highway.

In no time, she was pulling into the Target parking lot, and to her excitement, it wasn't nearly as packed as the last time she'd been there.

Parking, she locked her car and grinned—until she caught the line. Target had adjusted it this time, switching to a different entrance so she hadn't seen it at first. But it was there: dozens of people, maybe thirty in total, all waiting for the toy.

She took another step, then another, not really sure why or what she would do. Maybe she would just wait and see. Maybe they received a giant truckload. Maybe…

But then she scanned the crowd again, taking them all in one by one. The parents huddled together, the two moms teaming up together, the—

Kylie stopped cold, blinked once, then twice. His eyes were locked on her, his hands in his pockets. It was freezing out there, no warmer than thirty, and he was standing there in nothing more than a gray pullover. But that wasn't the most shocking thing about him being there. It was that he was first in line. First. Which meant he had to have arrived hours ago. He'd frozen there in that pullover for hours…all for her.

Her heart couldn't take it.

So instead of asking what he was doing there or making a joke or walking away for fear of what her next step might mean, she sped up. One foot, then another, the chill in the air forgotten, the Christmas music from her car still in her head, her eyes never leaving his.

"You…"

"Yeah."

"But that's…"

"I know."

Her heart pounded as the surge of emotions overcame her, and then in one more step, she was to him, her hands cradling his face as her lips met his.

A burst of sparks zipped through her, radiating out from her chest, while her mind went fuzzy. Brady went still at first, and then he smiled against her lips and pulled her closer, his arms wrapping around her. His lips were cold against hers and he tasted like cinnamon, and as his cold nose brushed against her cheek, the kiss deepening with his tongue sweeping inside her mouth, claiming her all over again, she had one thought and one thought alone: *finally.*

After far too short a time, Brady pulled back and ran his hands over her face, a giant question mark on his.

"I don't understand," he said. "I mean, I'm not complaining, but I'm not understanding. Where did this come from?"

Kylie shook her head and pulled him against her again. She unzipped her coat and forced his arms inside and around her so she could warm him. "You're freezing. How long have you been here?"

He shrugged. "Since about five, I guess. Maybe a little before."

Tears pricked her eyes as she took in his flushed face, his lips cracked from being out there so long. "You don't have a coat. What are you doing out here?"

"I saw the notification on your phone, and you were so worried with Franny. I couldn't help you, couldn't help her, but by God, I could come out here and stand in line for this toy. So, I told the nurse to let you know I was going and took off. I was the first in line."

A breath released slowly, and Kylie felt like an idiot. Of course he told the nurse. "The nurses switched shifts. Lauren left, so when you weren't there, I thought…"

Brady's gaze dropped. "You thought I broke another promise."

"I'm sorry."

His eyes flew back up to her. "You're sorry? I did this, Ky. Me. I never told you how much you meant to me back then. I didn't even talk to you about my school choices, what I wanted to do. Then I threw it at you that I was going halfway across the country, and I just assumed you'd go with me. I didn't even stop to ask you, to talk about it. It's my fault."

"No," Kylie said, shaking her head again. "I shouldn't have walked away. That's all I seem to be able to do any time things get bad. When I get scared. I run. Well, I don't want to run anymore. I just…I just want to be with you."

A slow smile curved his lips and he bent his head toward her. "I'm going to kiss you now, but seeing as how you did it first, I'm thinking there's permission here."

She laughed. "Yes, unlimited permission."

He kissed her, harder this time, the kiss saying everything they'd wanted to say for years now. They walked away from each other, but it wasn't over—their love hadn't ended.

The doors opened, and Kylie pulled away from him to find a man in a manager's shirt appear. "Good morning," he said to the crowd. "We've unpacked all our boxes and we received only one Real N Feel doll. It's a girl." His eyes then fell on Kylie and Brady. "Your daughter is going to be a happy little girl."

"Ah!" Kylie screamed and wrapped her arms around Brady again, neither of them even correcting him about the reason they were there for the doll.

"For the rest of you, I'm so sorry. I know the manufacturer is fighting to keep up with demand. We will receive them every day, and it is first come, first served, with each person able to purchase only one doll. Please try again tomorrow."

The crowd groaned from behind them and slowly dispersed, but Kylie and Brady were all grins. The manager motioned to the doors. "You can come on to customer service to purchase it."

"Thank you. Thank you so much," Kylie said.

"Thank him," the manager said. "He was here before me this morning."

Kylie eyed Brady, his hands still so cold. "I will never be able to thank you enough for this. You have no skin in this, yet you came out here for Ally and Rena."

"No," he said. "I came here for you. I messed up once, Ky. If you'll let me, I'll prove to you that I won't take you for granted again."

She grinned. "Second time's the charm?" She pulled out her credit card to buy the doll, when Brady waved her away.

"I've got this."

"But..."

"Let me do this."

Kylie rose onto her toes and kissed him again. She could get used to this.

Chapter 14

"Let me tell you, if you think I'm going to just lay up in this bed and let you tell me what to do all the time, you have another think coming." Franny glared at Kylie, who had just tucked her into her bed at home, turned on the TV to the Hallmark Channel so she could watch one of those Christmas movies she loved, and set a bottle of water beside her bed.

"I'm not trying to tell you what to do. I'm trying to take care of you. And to do what your doctor asked. And to ensure you live a few more days to put up with me."

Franny rolled her eyes. "I'd just as soon find my grave this second than follow that diet."

It was the same thing she'd said for the last three days, while they kept her in the hospital, running tests and getting her to the point where she could safely leave. Her blood pressure was off, which she claimed was because they wouldn't leave her alone and she was stressed out. She'd been tense and difficult the entire time, so very unlike Franny, but then it wasn't every day that one suffered a heart attack and had to listen over and over about how it was preventable.

"You have heart disease."

"So? Are you seriously going to stand there and tell me that by this point I wouldn't be riddled with some other disease if not this one? I can't live my life in fear of sickness, trying to prevent this thing from getting worse and hating every minute of it. God set my life's plan the moment he put me on this Earth. A little exercise ain't going to prevent my death."

Kylie exhaled slowly. "Maybe. Maybe not." It was an argument they'd had many times. Franny believed, like many Christians, that lives were set the moment we were born, every detail etched in some book up in Heaven.

But Kylie was more progressive in her beliefs. She thought God gave us this life, but that it was up to us to treasure it, take care of ourselves, and make the most of it.

"I'm not having this talk with you right now. It's my body. If I want cheesecake, by God I'm going to eat it."

"You realize you went from sane adult to insane old person in a matter of days, right?"

Franny pulled back, clearly offended. "You better take that back."

"You need to ask yourself what you would want for me. If I were in the hospital and the doctor gave me a strict diet to follow in order to keep me living, would you want me to follow it? Would you force me to follow it if needed to keep me here?"

At that Franny leaned back in her bed and crossed her arms, her face twisted in annoyance. "Where is the remote?"

Kylie fought back a smile and sat down beside her on the bed. "Right here. Do you need anything else?"

"Yes, you to go somewhere else. And don't even pucker that lip. You've been up under me every second of every day for half a week now. Don't you need to see that man that keeps coming by and grinning at you?"

"I haven't—"

"You have. And I'm tired of it."

Okay, so maybe there was some truth to what she was saying.

After she and Brady had left Target with the doll, they grabbed coffee and went immediately back to the hospital, only to find Franny awake and as ornery as ever. Three days later, those nurses were probably thanking God when Franny left.

Brady came by each day to check on them both, and it became apparent to Kylie that he cared about Franny, too. He tensed when Franny seemed in pain and rushed to her side every time she asked for something when he was there.

But now, Franny was back home, and according to her doctor, in good health, considering what she'd been through. Now she needed to work on her diet and general health to help ensure she didn't suffer another heart attack.

It was getting late, and Kylie was tired—exhausted, really. She loved the idea of getting a shower and going to bed, but then what if Franny needed something? Maybe she should sleep on the couch, just to be safe.

"Do you have your phone?" Franny asked.

A movie started up on the TV, something about "Jingles in Christmastown" or something. A mousy brunette was talking to what appeared to be her boss about needing a vacation, and he was telling her that retailers didn't offer vacation around the holidays.

"Yeah, why?" Kylie passed it over to her, her attention on the screen. In truth, she loved these Hallmark movies as much as Franny.

The mousy woman huffed and went back to her job in the shoe department. It appeared to be a major department store, and in typical holiday fashion, was filled with people.

"Good. Okay, can you come get her now?"

Kylie jerked back and glanced at her godmother. "Who are you talking to and when did you call them? I didn't even see you make a call."

Franny pressed a finger to her lips for Kylie to be quiet. *"Shh."* Then she grinned. "No, not you, sweetie. You heading over? All right, good. See you soon. Great, thanks, honey. Bye."

She handed the phone back to Kylie, then turned the volume up on the movie. "Oh, I love this one. It kind of has that Cinderella element to it, don't you think? Now, don't look at me like that. I know you watch them as much as I do."

Kylie glanced around like she'd walked into a different room—a different world. Maybe Franny's medication was doing freaky things to her head. "Um, did you or did you not just call someone?"

"I did."

"Care to tell me who?" Then Kylie realized that her brain wasn't working so well either, because she could just look at her calls. She picked up the phone and clicked for recent calls. "Why did you call Brady?"

The movie went to commercial, and Franny finally glanced over at her. "Because, I want him to take you away for a while so I can rest without you driving me crazy. Before you go, though, can you get me some popcorn?"

"Wait, what? And no, you can't have that gross butter-covered stuff."

"It might be bad for me, but it's delicious and you know it."

"You can have regular popcorn, no butter."

"What?" Franny pulled back in shock. "Who eats popcorn like that?"

"Plenty of people do. It's a—no, stop." Kylie waved her hands in the air. "You back up. What did you ask Brady to do?"

Just then the doorbell rang and Kylie glanced over to the bedroom door. "What, did he fly here?"

"He was close by."

"But I'm not going out. I need to be here for you."

"No. You have been there for me, and I'm fine. Doc said so herself. Now you need to go be there for you. But seeing as how you won't do that, and you prefer to be stubborn as all hell, I called in reinforcement."

The doorbell rang again and Kylie glanced down at the same junk clothes she'd been wearing earlier. Of course, Brady didn't care. But they were new again, and she liked the idea of impressing him, putting on a little bit of makeup, and dressing up a touch. Okay, so dark jeans instead of light jeans, but still. Sure, he'd seen her at the hospital in all kinds of different things, but that was different.

A knock came then, followed by a text on her phone.

"Honey, you better go answer that door before he leaves and goes over to Valerie's house instead. You know she's wanted him since birth. Don't give him a reason to go there."

"I...he's..." She pushed off of the bed, then pointed at her godmother. "I'm not done with you yet."

Franny grinned. "Whatever you say."

The house was dark as Kylie made her way out of the master bedroom, down the small hall and then into the open floor plan of the main level. They'd left the porch light on, and she could see Brady's' form through the glass inset in the wooden door. Her pulse picked up with each step. Why was she so nervous? This was a man who'd once known everything there was to know about her, been with her at her worst, seen her cry and scream and even vomit. Yet...all that felt like a movie she'd watched long ago and couldn't quite remember the ending. This was new, a chance at a redo. She didn't want to mess it up.

Drawing a long breath, she unlocked the door and swung it open. Brady's lips curved into a small smile when he saw her, and she tried to think of something clever to say, but instead all she could do was stare.

He'd had a work function and couldn't come to the hospital that morning, so she hadn't seen him since the night before. How a man could become more attractive in twenty-four hours was beyond her, yet there he stood, dressed in a button-down that he'd long since rolled to his elbows. Jeans and Converse completed his look, and the shoes reminded her so much of the boy she'd once known and loved that for a second she just stared at them.

"Converse."

"Yeah, I keep them in the car so I can change if I'm in work shoes."

"That's very you." She glanced up, taking in his shaved head. He looked so different, and yet as she met his eyes, startling blue cradled in full dark lashes, she couldn't help thinking that he hadn't changed at all.

"I'm sorry Franny called you. I'm fine, really."

He took a step toward her, took her hand in his. "I know that. But I'd like to take you to a movie anyway. I talked to Ms. Sally next door and she's going to come over and sit with Franny while we're gone."

"But I—"

"You are going!" Franny yelled from the bedroom and Kylie glared in that direction.

"She's stubborn."

"Not so unlike her goddaughter," Brady said. "But I agree with her. You need this."

"Yes, you need this. Now go." Ms. Sally from next door pushed her four-foot-eight self past Brady and Kylie and stopped in the foyer. She wore a robe and bedroom shoes, and her black hair was pinned back in rollers, a hairnet securing them in place. "I've got this, little girl. You go be young."

Twenty-eight didn't exactly register to Kylie as young, but she could tell by Sally's expression and her hand fixed to her robed hip that she wasn't going to hear another word about it.

"Sally, is that you?"

Sally spun around and cupped her mouth with one hand, then shouted back, "It's me, Fran! Trying to kick this kid of yours out of here!"

"Lord, she's still here?" Franny called back, and Kylie rolled her eyes.

"Right, so that's my signal," she said with a laugh. "You have my number, right?" she asked Sally, who took her turn to roll her eyes and then headed straight for the kitchen. "Grabbing some healthy crap for you, Fran, then I'll be right in there."

Kylie couldn't help but laugh, and knowing that Sally was a retired nurse made her feel better. She wouldn't allow Franny to have anything that wasn't on the approved list.

"Okay, so a movie?"

Brady closed the door and took Kylie's hand, leading her down the front porch steps. "We have two options, each starting in about twenty minutes."

A curious smile curved her lips. "I'm listening."

"Inappropriate comedy or action-adventure."

Immediately, Kylie bounced. "*Oooo!* What's the action-adventure? Let's go to that one."

Brady hit the unlock button on his car keys and walked around to open the passenger side door for Kylie. "Action it is, though I heard it's selling out everywhere."

"Uh oh."

He leaned inside the door and whispered in her ear. "Which is why I bought tickets online."

"You didn't. How would you know what I'd choose?"

Brady pulled back enough so she could see him clearly. "Because I know you, Ky. What's inside, the deep stuff, it doesn't change."

He kissed her easily, then walked around to get in, and all Kylie could think was that she hoped he was wrong. She was counting on her inner self changing, the deep wounds healing. Otherwise, she was doomed to repeat the mistakes from her past, and she couldn't do that to Brady.

Not this time.

By the time they reached the theater and stepped out of the car, a light snow had started to fall, and kids who had previously been in line with their parents were now running around on the sidewalk, trying to catch it in their mouths.

The parents stood nearby, watching and laughing, then trying to call their kids inside, all to no avail. What kid wanted to sit in a theater, forced by her parents to sit still and quiet, when they could scream and play in the snow? Of course, the snow wouldn't stick, but that didn't stop the magic it brought to the kids' imaginations.

Brady gripped Kylie's hand and pulled her to a stop. He was pensive as he stared down at her. Clearly, something was on his mind, and Kylie wondered if this was all a little too much, too fast for him—Franny's heart attack, Kylie admitting her feelings—her inability to be this close to him without aching to kiss him.

Gingerly, he plucked something from her hair. "Snowflake."

"Brady, I—"

He leaned in to kiss her, stealing her words as his lips performed their own version of magic. It took him a moment to pull away. "I'm sorry. It was just seeing you out here, snow all around us, it reminded me of another time."

Several of the people passing by had stopped to watch the children. There was something about snow in a place like a movie theater that made kids want to be silly. Kylie knew because this wasn't the first time she and Brady had been outside a movie theater with snow in the air, only that time school had been canceled and there were six inches on the ground. They'd just started whatever they were starting, and so when he'd come by her house and said he was taking her to a movie, she hadn't argued. She'd grinned ear to ear, grabbed her coat, and followed him to his truck. At the time, she would have followed him anywhere.

"I know. I was thinking about the same thing," she said. "It was the moment I knew you wanted more than friendship."

Brady laughed loudly, the sound rumbling from his chest to hers. "Make no mistake, sweetheart. I never had my sights on friendship." Then his expression turned serious, and he swallowed hard, his Adam's apple bobbing in the effort. "I think I loved you the moment I met you."

Kylie stilled, her emotions bubbling up, all words lost.

"Brady?"

Apparently, some didn't struggle with words. Or timing.

Sighing, Kylie took a step back to find Valerie had stopped outside the theater. She stood beside another woman, who likely went to their high school, but Kylie had never been a name person.

Brady released a slow breath, and Kylie fought back a grin. He seemed as aggravated at the interruption as her.

"Hey there," he said. "Seems a busy night here."

Valerie offered a grin, then her gaze slid from him to Kylie, and the smile dropped. "Hi, Kylie."

"Hi, it's good to see you."

Valerie nodded, and for the second time, Kylie thought she wasn't the villain that Kylie once assumed her to be. She was just another woman who fell for Brady. "Well, I'll see y'all later. Enjoy your movie." She followed her friend into the theater, stopping inside to peer out the window at Brady again before heading over to the ticket counter.

"Wow." Kylie shook her head, then laughed. "What in the world did you do to her?"

"Me?" he scoffed. "I just said hey."

"Not now, crazy. Before. In the past. Clearly, she's still not over it."

And now Brady scratched his head uncomfortably. "There might have been a date or two a long time ago. But we ended it as friends."

"*You* ended it as friends. She ended it with an ellipsis of things to come. I guess I can't say I blame her."

Brady opened the door for her and took her hand again as they walked inside. Framed movie posters covered the navy walls. Arcade games lined the back, while the ticket counter took up the left side, and refreshments occupied most of the center. A line to get into one of the movies ran the right-hand side of the theater. "So you're saying we ended with an ellipsis, too?"

The kids from outside came in, some by force, others with grumbles, but otherwise following their parents behind Kylie and Brady. One of the movie staffers scanned their tickets on Brady's phone, then told them which theater to go to.

"Not answering the question, I see," Brady whispered as they took their seats, but Kylie didn't know how to say what was on her mind.

To her, she wasn't the one who ended things, the one to keep the sentence—the relationship—open ended. He was. And revealing how often she'd checked her phone after that fateful day, how often she'd searched for him around school, how often she'd driven by his house, only to turn away before she reached the driveway for fear that he would recognize her car.

"For me, there was never an ellipsis. There was a period after your name, not because we had ended—but because my heart stopped at you."

Brady lifted the arm rest between them and tugged her closer, his lips finding hers as the lights to the theater dimmed and previews began.

She only hoped this time around they were on the same page. Her heart wouldn't survive Brady leaving her again. But he wasn't leaving.

Right?

Chapter 15

"Damn, I didn't realize you were this gone."

Brady shook his head, clearing the Kylie-infused daze he'd stepped into the moment he entered the shop, and eyed his brother, Charlie.

His brothers came by to check on things, which was another way of saying they wanted to make sure he was keeping his head in the game. Which he was...mostly.

"Don't know what you're talking about," Brady said as he adjusted the papers in front of him, including a note from Ally that a man had stopped by to see him, with a number below the name.

"We're talking about that infatuated look in your eye," Zac said.

"What?"

"You love her," the brothers said at the same time, and Brady had to turn around to keep from proving them right.

Because there it was again, the word that refused to leave his head. Holy hell, did he ever love this woman. The original feelings he'd felt before were still there, but something new had blossomed from that foundation, something deeper and more honest. This wasn't fun, careless love. This was experienced and full of all the realities that adulthood brings. Nothing would be easy, yet with her in his arms, all he could think was that whatever they faced, he could deal with it, so long as they were together.

A part of him wanted to tell her, but then he thought about how shocked she'd seemed when she saw him at Target. How a person could expect another person to always leave was beyond him. His family counted on one another and rarely disappointed. To never know what stable felt like must be hard, and though he'd seen it firsthand with her parents all those years ago, he'd never understood how deep that fear ran in her until that moment. She thought he'd left her, and the relief on her face was enough to make him want to prove to her over and over that he wouldn't leave. He was staying.

But proving that to someone would take time. So he would pocket the love card until she was ready to hear it and trust it. People threw around the word all the time. He wanted her to know that he didn't just mean it; he intended to put it into practice every day for as long as she would put up with him.

"Look, if there's nothing else you need, I got a few calls to make."

Zac eyed his watch, then clapped Charlie on the back. "I have to get to the farm. You going to Southern Dive?"

Charlie stretched his arms out behind him. "Meeting Lila at AJ&P for breakfast, then going over a few designs with the printer."

"T-shirts or marketing stuff?" Zac asked as Brady's attention drifted back over to Kylie. She was talking to a customer across the room who was waving his hands frantically as he spoke. Brady couldn't hear what the man was saying, but if his hands were any inclination, he was letting Kylie have it.

The protective side of him kicked in, and he held the counter to keep from walking over there to see what was up. He reminded himself that Kylie had always been able to handle herself, and that that was her side of the shop. Brady had no business involving himself.

Ally came up beside the pair then, and Kylie said something to her before Ally walked to the back.

"So, I need to check a few things and make those calls. See y'all later?"

"Yeah, later, brother," Zac said, then waved as he headed out, Charlie on his heels with his phone out, likely texting Lila that he was on his way.

Brady waited until they were out of sight, then headed to the back to ask Ally what was going on.

A grumbling sound of frustration hit his ears as soon as he passed through the swinging door. "What was that?" he asked.

Ally shot him a look and then bent back down to move around boxes on the Merrily side of the stockroom. "Stupid, self-righteous pond scum out there giving Kylie lip because an ornament on our website isn't in the store. She tried to explain to him that it's not a retail site where you can purchase things, that it's just for looks, but there was no reasoning with him. So now Kylie is having me pull out the ones she put away for the drawing later this month to see if that ornament is one of them. Big giant bull piece of sewer crawl."

A laugh broke from Brady's lips, and he tried to cover it with another laugh before Ally took that anger out on him. "Pond scum sewer crawl?"

"You got a better name?"

"Actually, I can think of a few. Want me to go save her?"

Ally sighed heavily. "No. As much as I want to gang up on the bully, she wouldn't want that. She's tougher than she looks."

"Yeah...she is."

Ally rummaged through another box before finally pulling out an ornament, holding it up high in the air, and shouting, "Got it!" Then she smiled to Brady before rushing back to join Kylie and the customer.

Brady knelt down and placed all the boxes Ally had removed from the shelf back into their rightful place, then scanned the storage room. The two sides were still in place, but Merrily had a few larger boxes labeled on his side and he had a few small boxes labeled on the shelving on Merrily's side. In no time, they'd interwoven the two, becoming a part of a whole instead of two separate spaces.

Which made Brady wish they could continue to operate like this, two in one building. But his brothers would never go for it, and they weren't wrong—Southern Dive needed more space. Still, the contract's end date was fast approaching, and Brady found himself wishing they could put it off a bit longer.

Deep in his thoughts, Brady went back out to Southern Dive & ETC's counter, grabbed the note Ally had left him, and dialed the number. As the phone rang, he watched Kylie hand over the wrapped ornament and the man smiling bright, then explained something to Kylie that had her cover her mouth with her hands, her eyes turning sad before she hugged him. Only Kylie could hug a person who had been yelling at her moments before.

"Good morning, Trent, Lock and Young," a male voice said. "How may I direct your call?"

Brady's gaze dropped to the note, curiosity swirling through him now. "Edward Young, please."

"Of course, may I tell him who is calling?"

"Brady Littleton."

"One moment please."

Turning around, Brady propped the phone on his shoulder and went to work opening his laptop and sorting through the online orders from the day before. There were twenty-two in all, nearly double the amount of daily orders they'd received a month ago. Business was booming, and with the Christmas rush, space was dwindling. Once again, he thought of the contract and felt a pang in his chest.

It was a few weeks away. He didn't need to worry about that right now.

"Brady," a booming voice said into the phone. "I'm so glad you called. My name is Edward Young. I met your brother, Charlie, at a conference a few weeks ago."

Okay, what did that have to do with him? "No problem at all. What can I do for you?"

"I think the better question is what can I do for you and Southern Dive."

More and more people filtered into the shop, all crowded around an activity center Kylie had set up for people to paint glass ornaments. So far, she'd had an activity going every day, each one drawing a larger crowd. From kids to adults and the elderly, each table and chair were full. She had started with one table and six chairs. Now she had three tables set up, imposing more and more on Brady's side of the shop, but he couldn't bring himself to care.

"I'm not sure I understand," Brady said into the phone, his attention on Kylie and the smile that never left her face during these activities.

"My company is an investment firm, and we would like to invest in Southern Dive. I have worked up an expansion plan to help you and your brothers take your business to the next level. There are towns all over the country that would love to have a shop like yours, and I'm betting you've even noticed certain regions order online more often than others."

Brady leaned back against the counter. He had noticed. Florida, coastal South Carolina and North Carolina, places with interest in fishing and outdoor living.

"What would your company get out of this deal?"

"We would help you franchise the business, and in turn, negotiate a percentage ownership. Of course, one of you would help each business start up, spend six months or a year or more traveling between them to ensure everything goes as planned. It would be our money, but your business."

One of them traveling between locations. A year or longer? Zac and Charlie both had families, wives and children, which meant…it would fall on him if they agreed to take the investor's offer.

Once again, his gaze drifted to Kylie. They were just starting again. How would she feel about him leaving for a year? Or traveling more days than he'd be home?

A sinking feeling set in, weighing him down.

"Thank you for the chat, Edward. I will discuss this with my brothers, and we will call you later this week."

"Sounds like a plan, but please consider our offer seriously. We can make you all very wealthy men."

I'm wealthy enough, Brady thought.

"Thank you. We appreciate your interest. Expect a call by the end of the week."

They hung up, and Brady dropped his head.

"Wow, did someone die or something?"

Brady jerked upright and spun around to find Kylie standing there, that smile still planted on her face. "What? No, it was nothing."

"It didn't look like nothing. You seemed all tense." Concern took over her face and she reached out for his hand. "Everything okay?"

Here was his opportunity. He could tell her about the investor, what it might mean, lay it all out here now. That was the mistake he had made before—not telling her, not involving her. But his brothers didn't even know about this yet, and it might be nothing. He hated the idea of getting her upset when the brothers might very well decide to turn down the offer.

"Nah, seriously, it was nothing," he found himself saying, but even as the words left his mouth he wished he could freeze time, rewind, and do it all over again.

Kylie grinned. "Good. Well, I better get back. Want to grab lunch later?"

"Lunch sounds perfect."

Brady watched her walk away, that bad feeling inside him growing stronger with each step. "Hey, Ky."

She turned around. "Yeah?"

He took in the shimmer on her cheeks, the sparkle in her eyes, and how different this look was from the one she wore at the hospital after Franny's heart attack. He couldn't throw something like this at her now. So instead of telling her the truth, he said, "Captain Jack's for lunch?"

"Cheeseburger? You know it." She blew him a kiss, then rejoined the others around the activity tables, and Brady dropped his head again.

Maybe this was nothing, but deep down, he knew he was lying to himself. Southern Dive had a franchise opportunity. A life-changing opportunity. His brothers would be thrilled.

And he would have to leave Kylie...again.

Chapter 16

Kylie tiptoed into Franny's room to find her already sound asleep. She edged around to the side of her bed and watched the woman who was more a mother to her than her own mother sleep.

The heart attack had been scary and was a wake-up call to her in more ways than one. Life was precious, and living in fear wasn't living at all. A part of her feared what falling for Brady again could do to her if he decided to end things, but then, she wasn't exactly singing-and-dancing-in-the-halls happy before. Committing to Brady again tested Kylie's deepest fears, but the risk, so far, had been more than worth it.

Carefully, Kylie brought Franny's quilt up and over her, then turned off the TV—another Hallmark movie. Then she turned off the light and went on into the kitchen for a late-night snack, but she wasn't hungry. She was tired, yet too keyed up to sleep.

A part of her wanted to go over to see Brady, but he had a weekly dinner with his brothers, and she didn't want to impose on that. The Littleton family was a close-knit group, and though Kylie had once felt like a part of it, the brothers deserved to have their weekly dinner to stay close and take care of that relationship.

Stretching, Kylie walked on up the stairs and turned on the water in her bath, waited for it to warm, then plugged the drain and added in a few bath bombs and relaxing bubble bath. She went back into her room to grab some PJs when a soft knock at her window caused her to startle.

Spinning, eyes wide, she faced the window, and then a slow smile took over her face. She bit her lip and went to the window, unlocked it, and raised it up. "You trying to scare me to death?"

Brady crossed his arms and leaned against the edge of the house beside the windows. A flash of him as an eighteen-year-old in that same pose hit her, and the smile widened.

"I didn't want to knock on the front door and risk waking Franny."

"You're supposed to be at dinner with your brothers."

He shrugged and cocked his head, a crooked smile pulling up one side of his mouth. "I was. Then I realized that I'd forgotten something the last time I saw you, so I came over."

"Forgot something, huh?" Kylie pushed the screen out and stood back and waved her arm for him to come in. He bent down and stepped one foot in, then balanced and pulled in the other, and Kylie had to steady him to keep him from falling. They laughed.

"Yeah, not eighteen anymore."

She grinned. "No, you're not." She bit her lip again as she peered up at him. He was dressed in a button-down and dark jeans. Scruff covered his strong jaw, and his blue eyes were so clear and bright it was like God made that color just for him.

"You were saying you forgot something."

"Oh, right." And then in one step, his right hand slid through her hair, cradling her head, and his lips came down on hers. The faint taste of beer hit her tongue, and though she knew he would never drive intoxicated, she could tell he was in a good mood. His body pressed closer, and the kiss deepened, his tongue sweeping inside and reminding her that no one kissed like Brady Littleton.

Rising onto her toes, she draped her arms around his neck, closed what little distance remained between them, and felt the telltale evidence of the kiss's effect on him on her thigh. Brady pulled back and shook his head. "That's not getting old anytime soon." Then his brows pulled together and he eyed the bathroom. "Is that water running?"

"Oh!" Kylie dashed into the bathroom and turned off the bath. Bubbles floated along the top, and she bent down to let out some of the water when Brady came up behind her and wrapped his arms around her waist.

"Bath?"

"I couldn't sleep." She caught his eye in the mirror. "Seems a shame to waste the water."

Their gazes held. "Agreed. After all, there's people in the world who would kill for this much water."

"And it's an awfully big bath," Kylie said, her voice dropping to a whisper. "Probably even room for two."

Brady swallowed, then ducked his head until his lips found Kylie's neck. He kissed a trail from her ear to her shoulder, then slowly spun her around. "Are you asking me to take a bath with you?"

"I am asking you to take a bath with me."

That crooked grin she loved returned. "All right then." He ran his fingers along the edge of her shirt, then trailed them against her stomach. Goose bumps rose across her skin. Then he eased the shirt up and over her head, dropping it easily to the ground, leaving her in just a bra and black leggings. Immediately, his eyes met hers, watching for her reaction, but she wasn't afraid or nervous. It was like she'd spent the last ten years lost, searching for a home she didn't have, only to come to this point and discover he'd been her home all along.

Kylie went to work unbuttoning each of the buttons of his dress shirt, then pushed it off his shoulders and he shrugged it off until it dropped. Like always, he wore a white T-shirt under the button-down, and like always, Kylie preferred him in this look—jeans and a T.

Kylie ran her hands under the T-shirt and over the defined contours of his abs before pulling the shirt off and over his head, then dropping it with hers. Her eyes drank him in, each cut of his chest, down to the sharp V and trail of blond hair from his belly button that disappeared into his jeans. Suddenly, the intensity building between them sparked into a flame and all thought left her as she went for his jeans, unfastened them, and pushed them to the ground.

Kicking out of them, Brady stood before her, in only boxers, and Kylie slowly pushed her leggings down and off until she, too, was in only underwear. A thoughtful person would have sensed this as a possibility and wore something frillier, but instead, she stood before him in a basic black thong and black bra.

They stared at each other for a moment, taking in all the changes. Brady had always been fit, but Brady the boy was a much smaller version of Brady the man. The lean muscles of his teenage years had morphed into thick, defined strength, and it wasn't lost on her how easily he could slip into one of the Marvel movies, his body every bit as impressive as theirs.

"You're bigger now," she said, then felt her cheeks flush at the stupid comment. But all a sudden she felt nervous.

Brady took her hand and pulled her closer. "If possible, you're more beautiful." He kissed her, and as his hands went around to the clasp of her bra, she pushed aside her nerves. He unclasped her bra and it dropped to the ground with the rest of their clothes.

His hand glided easily over her breast as he kissed her again, cupping her gently, then he bent down and pressed his lips to the swell of her breast and she arched her back, moaning softly, before he took her nipple into his mouth.

Kylie edged his boxers down and he stepped of them, his length before her, and Brady slipped off her thong, then led her to the bath.

She sank into the bubbly, hot water, and Brady eased in behind her. His fingers ran down her breasts, over her stomach, then slowly down her legs, causing her to arch against him. Then he brought his hands slowly back up, stopping at her heat, and Kylie thought she would lose her mind.

He slipped a finger inside her, and Kylie turned her head, bringing him closer, their mouths connecting as he continued to tease her.

Unable to handle it any longer, Kylie balanced her hands on the edge of the tub and turned around until she straddled him. It took everything in her not to pull him inside her, the want too great. Bubbles covered his chest and hers, and Brady set up, stroking her right nipple before bringing his mouth down around it and sucking her into his mouth. She bit her lip to keep from crying out and rocked against him, causing him to groan against her as she rocked still harder.

"I need you inside me," she breathed.

"Not without protection."

Kylie moaned again as he kissed her other breast. "Please."

Brady eased her off him and out of the water, grabbed a towel, and as quickly as possible dried them both off. He grabbed his jeans and pulled out a condom from his wallet, then picked her up and carried her into her room.

Laying her on the bed, Brady stared down at her, his eyes full of want as he tore open the condom and rolled it on. Then he crawled up her, stopping to press a kiss to the inside of her thigh, her hip, then a hot kiss to her mound, gliding his tongue over her before kissing his way up her stomach and over each of her breasts.

Kylie bucked against him, all control lost, and then he drove deep inside her, bringing them back to center, and to how much this moment meant to them. He slowed down then, and Kylie felt her emotions swirling with her hormones, their eyes locking, until he secured his mouth over hers again, the kiss harder this time, saying all the things they weren't ready to say.

She came in a rush of intensity and sparks and spasms while Brady released inside her, and all Kylie could think was nothing in her life had ever felt as perfect as this moment.

Chapter 17

Brady opened his door and immediately bent down to kiss Kylie. His skin went tingly, his chest soaring, and he smiled against her lips. "I will never get tired of kissing you."

She rose up and kissed him again. "I hope not. And wow, what is that smell?"

Brady grinned as he led her into the kitchen, where he'd been slaving over lamb chops, roasted asparagus, and seasoned potatoes.

"This looks amazing," she said.

"Are you ready to eat?"

Kylie sat down at the table and Brady brought her plate of food, then wine and water, just to be safe. They'd had sex days before, and yet, he was nervous.

Dimming the lights, he made his own plate and took the seat beside her. "How was your day?"

"Sorry, I have to try this first," she said, taking a bite, then moaning in a way that made him happy in more ways than one.

"Good?" he asked, taking a sip of his wine.

"Ridiculously good. Seriously, you could have your own show or something. Lord. I need to have you teach me so Franny can stop grimacing at me every time I try to make her something."

Brady laughed, and they settled into eating. "How was your day?"

"Good. Busy. The shop's busier than it's ever been. I'm starting to wonder if women are coming in to shop for Christmas decorations or to see the new hottie at the other half of the store." She winked at him as she continued to work on her plate. "But yeah, I'm exhausted."

Brady focused on his plate, took another bite to finish up his meal, then wiped his mouth with his napkin and leaned back in his chair to look at her. "Then maybe you should stay here tonight."

She glanced up. "Stay here."

"We could do the movie thing, and if you think this is good, just wait until you try my eggs benedict."

"So what you're offering is a slumber party of sorts. Are we going to paint each other's nails, too?"

"Paint nails, ravage each other's bodies, whatever you want."

She choked on a laugh and reached for her water. "That's a thought."

But Brady wasn't laughing. He was serious. He would do whatever she wanted, say whatever she wanted. He wanted her to stay in his house, in his bed. It seemed like forever ago that she'd first came there, and he remembered feeling attacked, like she'd invaded his world. Now he was desperate for her to be here.

Kylie stood up, reached for his plate and then hers, and went around to the sink, Brady trailing behind her. He slipped his hands around her waist and kissed her neck as she rinsed the plates. "I told you last time—you're a guest."

"And I told you that I can put the plates in the dishwasher."

"So, movie?"

Kylie opened up the dishwasher and set the plates inside, then spun around in his arms. "Or..." She rose onto her toes, her body pressed against his, and kissed him with a new intensity. Their tongues tangled as his hands slipped through her silky strands.

He gripped her hips and lifted her up onto the counter for better access, and the kiss deepened, until Kylie released, her breath labored. "I don't want to watch a movie."

"No?" he asked, his eyes locked on hers.

"No."

And then in one quick move, he pulled her off the counter and looped her legs around his waist. They kissed as he carried her down the hall, then laid her on his bed, her curls feathering out all around her head. No one had ever looked more beautiful.

Brady took his time helping her remove her shirt, her jeans, her bra, and then stepped back to look down at her as he removed his own clothes, their eyes locked the entire time. How had he ever lived without her?

Responsibility called, and he went to his nightstand to grab a condom, tore it open, and rolled it on. Then he returned to her, but this was none of the quickness of the other night. No, this time, he intended to take his time. Slowly, he slipped inside her, and they kissed as they began to move, each push insane bliss and agony all at the same time.

He opened his eyes to look at her, watched as her face tensed with her orgasm, and the words were right there—*I love you. I love you so much that I don't know how I breathe when you're not around.*

But instead of saying it, he finished and pulled her against him, holding her close. "I'm glad you're here."

"Me, too." She turned in his arms, kissed his lips, and whispered in his ear. "Again."

Chapter 18

Christmas Eve came, and Kylie stared around Merrily Christmas, her heart full. Though they hadn't reached the sales goal she'd hoped for, sales for November and December had surpassed the previous three years' sales in those months, last year by more than thirty percent. Which had to be enough to keep the store going.

"Okay, I'm out of here," Ally said, a giant grin on her face, the wrapped Real N Feel doll in her arms. She'd decided to keep it at the shop instead of hiding it in her house, and had swung by moments before to pick it up before heading home to prepare for Santa's visit. "I could kiss that man of yours for this."

Kylie laughed. "Not sure your husband would be too happy about that, but I'll be sure to give him one for you. I'm glad Rena will get her Christmas wish."

"Will you be getting yours tonight?" Ally wiggled her eyebrows, and they both laughed.

"Go on before you drink more egg nog and I have to drive you home."

The women hugged, and Kylie locked the front door behind her friend before walking around to turn off the lights. Brady would be there any second to pick her up for his family's Christmas dinner, and to be honest, she was more than a little bit nervous.

Years ago, she viewed the Littleton home like her own, and spent many nights there having dinner and listening to the Littletons talk and laugh at the dinner table. It reminded her how rarely her own parents found time to be at the table. She was an outsider in every way, and yet never once did they make her feel like one.

"Whatup buttercup?"

A slow smile curled Kylie's lips as she turned to find Brady leaning against the back wall, keys in hand. She hadn't heard him enter over the Christmas music still streaming from the speakers.

"Hey there, I didn't hear you come in."

"I'm good like that," he said, winking. Then he pushed off the wall and started for her. His gaze drifted up and he pointed over her head to the mistletoe hanging above them. "Rules and all." He bent down and pressed a kiss to her lips. A bubbly feeling swirled through her stomach as goose bumps danced across her skin.

"Every time," she said, feeling suddenly light.

"What?"

"The butterfly feeling. Still hits me every time."

Brady leaned in and kissed her again. "Me, too." They remained close for a moment longer, taking each other in, before he pulled away. "All right, Mom texted me three times with the time and what we needed to bring, so we better get to it."

"Sure thing. I just need to grab one thing." Kylie darted over to the counter, dropped down, and pulled out the ornament she'd ordered for Mrs. Littleton. Then she opened one of Merrily's gift bags and started to slip it inside, when Brady spoke up.

"What's that?" Brady asked, coming near.

She shrugged. "Just a little gift for your mom." Kylie held it out. It was a hand-painted ornament of a mom reading to three boys. The word "Mother" crested the top of the ornament.

Brady stared at the ornament for a long time before finally glancing over to Kylie, and she thought maybe he didn't like it, when he said, "You realize you're going to be the favorite now."

"My plan all along," she said with a wink.

Slipping the ornament into the small bag, Kylie fluffed up the tissue paper inside, then adjusted the tiny Christmas tree that hung from the handles. The shop smelled like Christmas—all cinnamon and cookies and candles guaranteed to conjure the spirit within you. She hated to close the shop that night, knowing it might be its last Christmas. But she was learning that she couldn't be afraid of the "what ifs" in life. She had to press forward, take chances, and hope for the best.

"You all right?" Brady asked.

Kylie nodded, grabbed her purse, and then tucked the present inside. "Yeah, I'm good. Great actually." She slipped her arm through his. "Let's go."

The drive over to the Littletons' house was peaceful. Christmas music played from the radio, cars drove past, some honking a hello. It hadn't snowed in Crestler's Key since the night at the movie, but the air felt wintery and cold, and though Franny hadn't wanted to come to dinner, Kylie assured her that she would bring her home a plate—all heart healthy.

"You okay over there?" Brady asked for the second time since they'd gotten in the car.

Kylie smiled. "Yes, I'm sorry. I was just thinking about Franny. I hate that she didn't want to come to dinner."

"Do you want to skip and go home instead? I can let my parents know. They'll understand."

"No, it's okay. She insisted we go, which is her way of saying she wants a little alone time. Which is fine. I just don't want her to get lonely during that alone time, ya know?"

Brady eyed his watch. "How about we stay for an hour or so then head over with food? She can have the time she needs, but not so much time that she feels lonely."

"I'd hate for you to miss out on your family time."

"Trust me," he said with a laugh, "I'll be ready to get away from my brothers almost as soon as we get there."

"Why is that?"

Suddenly, the joking smile dropped from Brady's face, and he looked ahead again. "Just work stuff. No big deal."

It sounded like a big deal, but she and Brady were just growing close again. She didn't feel comfortable prying into things between him and his brothers.

They turned right down the next street, and one more turn would have them at Brady's parents' house. Christmas lights twinkled from several of the homes as they passed, some homes going as far as to have blow-up characters and reindeer in their yards. The whole thing felt like something out of a movie.

Brady parked the car in the Littletons' driveway behind a handful of other cars, a few she recognized as his brothers', but there were a few she didn't recognize. The knot in her stomach tightened.

"Big party."

Slowly, he ran his hand over her leg, then squeezed her knee. "You know everyone here."

"Like how much knowing are we talking about here? People that knew us before?"

He cocked his head. "A mix, but mostly, yes. That was all a long time ago. People forget, and besides, most blamed me." He winked, and Kylie laughed in return, though it didn't ease the nervousness wreaking havoc on her insides.

"Yeah, I'm not buying that for a second. Family supports family." *And small towns never forget*, she thought, but she didn't say it out loud.

Back then, Kylie had been so certain that she was doing the right thing, that Brady had lied and didn't care and would break her heart. Only now had she realized that she was the one to break his heart.

Of course he should have told her he was applying to colleges out west. He should have said that he wanted a career that couldn't happen in a tiny town like Crestler's Key.

But he didn't.

Shaking her head, she put on a smile and reminded herself that it was Christmas. Everything was fine, no, great. And they were together again, everything on the table now, honesty the common denominator that hadn't been there before. They knew what to expect of each other. What could go wrong?

Brady grinned back, then kissed her hand and opened his car door. "But I'd stay away from Aunt Willow if I were you."

"What? What did you say to Willow?"

"Nothing. Nothing at all." He raced up the steps, Kylie chasing after him, but before she could force him to dish, the front door opened.

"I'm going to get you for this. Expect pain," Kylie whispered as Zac's daughter, Carrie-Anne, stood in the doorway, beaming at Brady. She launched into his arms, and he hugged her tight before she went back inside.

Then Brady leaned in closer to Kylie. "Can this pain be of the bedroom variety? 'Cause I think I can get behind that. Unless you're wanting to be behind." He pulled back, his eyebrows raised in mock seriousness. "In that case, we'll need to discuss terms. Maybe a safe word or two."

Kylie burst out laughing, and he pulled her close. "See, there's the smile I love."

Their eyes locked on the word, but neither said anything. Instead, Brady's mom came rushing toward them, and hugged Kylie, then kissed her cheek.

"Child, I swear, you're more beautiful now than you were when you were younger, and you were a goddess before." Then she shot her son a look. "You better take care of this sweet girl. I don't want to get used to this face again, only to have it leave me."

Brady stared at Kylie. "Don't worry, Mom. I've got it this time."

She patted his cheek, then hugged him. "Good, and Merry Christmas."

"Merry Christmas," he said.

His mom pulled back, her face tense as she lifted her head a bit, then sniffed the air. "What is that smell?" Then her eyes went round. "Cripes! That's my apple pie." She scurried off, Kylie fighting back giggles.

"Like old times," she said.

"I told you. Nothing's changed here. Or for me."

"Brady!"

He whipped around to find his brothers rushing toward him, both grinning a bit too wide. "I see y'all have gotten into Dad's scotch."

"Nah," Charlie said. Then he laughed. "All right, maybe a little. Now, come end the debate. Dad and Zac said it was Coop Blackson who caught that TD pass that won state when you were a senior. But I told him it was Trey Long."

"Oh, sorry. Hey, Kylie." Charlie kissed her cheek, and Zac hugged her hello.

"It was Trey."

"See," Charlie said, pushing Zac playfully. "Your memory's shit, older brother." Then he motioned for Brady to follow them. "Come on, we're out back."

Brady eyed Kylie. "Nah, I'll just hang—"

"Go," she said. "I'll be fine here. It's not my first time with this crowd."

He hesitated, and she pushed him on. "Go, you know your dad won't believe Charlie. And yes, it was Trey," she added, causing the brothers to all laugh.

"Are you sure?"

"One hundred percent. Go."

Kate came over then, swooping Kylie away, and Brady followed his brothers out onto the back deck. They had a fire going in the fire pit, and several of his family members and friends of the family circled it to keep warm.

"There you are," Dad said as the brothers came near. "This boy thinks old Trey caught that State winner, but I told him it was—"

"It was Trey," Brady said, and his dad's face froze, causing all three of the brothers to burst into laughter.

It felt good to be there, surrounded by family, Christmas in the air, Kylie inside. Everything in his life had finally clicked into place.

The men continued to reminisce on some of the brothers' greatest sports moments in high school and college before Zac took a long pull of his beer and bumped Brady's shoulder. "Forgot to tell you that we have a meeting set up with that investor after the new year. I didn't think we could all swing it before. You okay with the Tuesday after, nine o'clock?"

And there was the reminder that Brady didn't have it all figured out, not yet.

"Yep, the date's good, but we'll need to go over the terms some more. I'm not game with being gone all the time if we do this."

"Do what?" Dad asked.

Charlie piped up then. "Remember I told you about that investor wanting to franchise Southern Dive? He called, and we have a meeting set up to talk out the details."

"Wow," Dad said, clearly impressed, and Brady felt that old urge to please his family coming to the surface. "So what's the plan there?"

Zac shrugged. "Not sure yet. We were thinking we would all three keep an eye on the construction, but Brady would travel out to each one, train the staff, and get it started. Probably would take a year or so."

Dad's eyebrows pulled together as he faced Brady. He'd always been able to read Brady's thoughts better than his brothers. "Are you okay with being gone a year?"

"You're leaving?"

All the blood drained from Brady's face at the voice coming from behind him. Slowly, he turned around to find Kylie frozen in place, her eyes wide like she was a deer in headlights and didn't know what to do.

"Time to eat!" Mom called from inside, and before he could say something to Kylie, to explain that he hadn't made any commitments yet, she turned and went back inside.

"You didn't tell her?" Zac asked, but Brady pushed on, eager to try to talk this out before they were seated at dinner and there was nothing he could do.

He walked up behind her as she stood with the rest of his family, waiting to hear how his mom would divide up seating for this many people. "Please don't freak out. This isn't a big deal."

"You being gone a year isn't a big deal?"

"I haven't agreed to anything yet. Nothing has been agreed upon yet. And even if it happened, it wouldn't be a year away. I would take small business trips as needed over the course of a year."

Kylie stared ahead. "Why didn't you tell me?"

"I...I don't know. It's all up in the air and I didn't want you to worry over nothing."

"I get it." But by the chill coming off her and the tension in her spine, she didn't get it at all. He needed to defuse this quickly, before her mind did its thing and there was no bringing her back.

"Can we go outside to talk?"

She drew a breath and released it slowly. "It's fine. We can talk about it when we leave."

But Brady knew there was nothing fine about it.

He scanned the room, took in Zac with Sophie, Carrie-Anne, and their son, Connor. Zac said something he couldn't hear and the kids laughed, while Sophie play-hit him in the stomach. The whole encounter seemed natural and easy, the way a family should be. Then he glanced to the opposite side of the room, where Charlie stood with an arm around Lila, who was holding their daughter, Violet, both smiling at the little girl like everything was made right in their lives the moment she was born.

Brady wanted that kind of happiness, but he didn't want it with just anyone—he wanted his smiling forever to be with Kylie. He needed to reassure her that no matter what, the new business didn't mean he was going anywhere permanently.

"Okay," Mom said, clapping to get everyone's attention. "Littleton kids, I have you and your families in the dining room." She pointed to Kate, Zac, Charlie, and then Brady. "Get going so I can see the rest of the group."

The brothers grinned at each other and started away. Brady took Kylie's hand and whispered in her ear, "Don't let this upset you. We'll talk about it, see what's best. Okay?"

She nodded, but still she wasn't looking at him. She hadn't looked at him since she heard that he might be leaving.

Mom's voice carried as they walked out of the common room, around the kitchen, and into the large dining room. The smell of roast turkey and dressing and mac and cheese mixed with a variety of pies, and not for the first time, Brady thought that his mother had outdone herself.

Zac took the head of the table without thinking, but instead of Charlie taking the other end, he nodded for Brady to go there. Hesitating, he took the seat, and Kylie sat beside him, then the rest of the clan filled in the extra seats of the twelve-seat table. His mom had set up a small table in the corner of the room for children, and the littlest kids squealed as they took seats and found activity sets there for them—crayons and coloring books, puzzles and other things to entertain them.

"Kylie, how's Franny doing?" Lila asked. "Merrily was always one of my favorite shops when I was little. I hated to hear about her heart attack."

Kylie smiled appreciatively. "She's doing a lot better. Fighting me on dietary restrictions, but she's doing great. Her last checkup was very good, so we're keeping on."

"That's great. Is she going to keep the shop going then?"

All at once, the table went quiet, and Brady shot Charlie a look, who intervened with a laugh. "Lila's been hanging out with Sophie too much. Makes her ask inappropriate things."

The table erupted as Sophie glared at Charlie. "I don't say inappropriate things. I'm just forward."

"That's one way to describe it," Zac joked, and the table relaxed again. All except Kylie, who was staring at her empty plate like she wanted to be anywhere but there.

Mom brought around trays of food and placed them in the center of the table, then smiled with pride at her family. "Thank y'all for being here," she said. "It means the world to me." Her eyes fell on Kylie and her smile brightened. Brady hadn't realized until that moment that maybe he wasn't the only one who had missed her. He needed to fix this. But how?

"Want me to help make your plate?" he asked, only to receive a look like he'd lost his mind. "What I mean was—I..."

Kylie placed her hand on his and offered the first real smile he'd seen since she overheard that he might be leaving. "Honestly, I'm fine. It's Christmas. Let's enjoy it." She took a dish that Kate had passed her way, and they settled into handing off trays and eating. But Brady couldn't shake the feeling that with Kylie, he would always be one step forward and three steps back.

Could he take living that way? He wasn't sure.

Chapter 19

"Yes! Yes, yes, yes!"

Kylie jumped out of her chair and bopped on her toes, clapping her hand like she'd lost her mind. Maybe she had. She checked the number again, then screamed out again.

"Um, you drink from Franny's crazy punch again?" Ally asked as she set down a box of spring goodies Kylie had ordered just in case the shop succeeded in hitting the numbers she agreed upon with Brady. And they were close. Dangerously close. So close that if Brady allowed her to include one extra week of sales, they would hit it.

"Check this out," Kylie said, handing over the sales report for December. Immediately, Ally screamed out, too.

"Is that for real? Are you telling me I might have a job after the new year?"

Kylie beamed. "It's amazing, right? We killed it. Absolutely killed it."

"But didn't you agree to sell three thousand more? Isn't that what the contact says?" Ally eyed the report again, and Kylie shrugged.

"I did. But we could sell that in a week if we tried, especially with all the holiday discounts and people wanting to scoop things up for next year."

"But you only have two days based on the contract terms."

"I know, but surely we could have a few extra days."

Ally drew a long breath and started back for the box she'd been unpacking.

"What?" Kylie asked.

"I don't know. It just seems like the Littletons are pretty strict about business. What makes you think they'll give you an extra week when if we can't deliver in two days, the contract says we lost?"

"Who lost?" Brady called from across the room, and Kylie shook her head at her friend before turning around and beaming at him.

"Nobody lost. Just I have some numbers from December that I'm pretty excited about."

It had been a week since that awkwardness at Christmas and it had taken her nearly that long to let it go. Sure, she pretended that everything was okay. She wanted it to be okay. Brady said he wasn't going anywhere, and even if they did the franchise thing, he'd only travel occasionally. So it wasn't a big deal.

Only, it felt like a big deal. The whole thing reminded her of all the years her dad traveled while her mom fought to do any and everything to stay busy—and away from her. Neither of them could stand the other for too long, and honesty was as big of a joke as the word family.

But Brady wasn't her dad, and she wasn't her mom. They were creating their own story. "That's awesome! So you hit your numbers?"

Kylie walked around the boxes that Ally now had scattered on the floor and wandered over to where Brady was standing. He paused midway to opening his laptop. "Why does it look like you're trying to butter me up?"

She bit her lip and contemplated what to do. The last thing she wanted was to use their relationship to get him to give her the extra week. That wasn't the sort of person she was, but at the same time, it was one little week. Couldn't she ask? Wouldn't she have asked if he were someone else?

Yes, most certainly she would. But there was a definite icky feeling about it, and she considered calling Franny to get her opinion before going there. After all, this was her shop, not Kylie's, even if inside Kylie felt like she'd put her whole heart into it since she was a little girl.

A curious grin curved Brady's lips and he glanced from Kylie to Ally. "What isn't she telling me?"

Ally threw up her hands. "I'm not getting involved in this. But I will say that I have a little girl, and she needs me to have this job."

Brady stood up taller then and turned toward Kylie. "Why is Ally guilting me with the mom card?"

"Hey, it's mommy card. Get it right," Ally called, but the moment had grown tense now. It wasn't the right time. She needed to go over things with Franny's accountant. Figure out if her numbers were accurate, and then she'd need to talk to Franny's lawyer and see if there was any wiggle room in the contract. But see, all that runaround felt icky, too, when the man who controlled it all stood before her and bore the title boyfriend.

"Can I say something, and you think about it without responding right now?"

It was still early morning, the shop doors locked, so they didn't have to worry about customers coming in to witness the tension rolling around in the air.

But why should it be this tense? It was a question, right? One little question, and he could say whatever. It didn't have to change anything between them either way. Right?

Kylie chewed her thumbnail, a habit she'd never had before. Tentatively, Brady reached out and pulled her hand away from her mouth, linked his fingers through hers, and took a step closer to her.

"What is it, Ky?"

"I need a week," she blurted.

His eyebrows pulled together in confusion. "Uh, not following you here."

Sighing, Kylie pressed on, with clarity this time. "I have the December report, and it's amazing. It's the best month we've had in years."

A relieved expression crossed his face and he pulled her close, hugging her. "That's fantastic. I knew you could do it."

"But." Kylie leaned away so Brady could see her face. "We're three thousand short of the contract, and I don't think I can hit that in two days. I need an extra week. One week. To hit the goal."

His face fell, and she knew even before he spoke that wasn't going to get the week. "Ky..."

"Your brothers."

"I promised them that I wouldn't let emotions get into this, that I would stick to the contract."

"Of course," she said, swallowing hard. She'd never been as good as Brady at keeping her emotions out of things. "And that's what you should do."

"That's what you would tell me to do if we were talking about anyone other than Franny."

No, actually, I wouldn't, Kylie thought. They were close to everyone in the town. She would tell him to give the person the week, see what happened. But she couldn't say that to him.

"Maybe."

Brady opened his mouth to say something else to convince her, but then a knocking on the store window had them both glancing over.

Zac and Charlie stood outside, with Zac pointing at his watch, then waving for Brady to hurry up.

"Sorry, I have to run to a meeting."

"With the investor, right?" Kylie asked, and though he stood right in front of her, she couldn't make herself look at him. Brady had always cared so much about succeeding in his family's eyes that she wondered if they could ever truly see eye-to-eye on the things that mattered. Life was about more than money and titles.

"Ky, look at me."

She glanced up, her face even.

"Everything is going to be okay." His brothers knocked on the window again, and he kissed her cheek before waving to them that he was coming. "We'll figure it out."

"Okay," she said, but inside she was thinking: *Before or after you put my family out of business?*

Chapter 20

Brady sat at the conference room table, his brothers seated beside him, and Ryan, the investor, sat across from them. They'd spent the last hour talking about everything Trent, Lock and Young, Ryan's company, could do for Southern Dive, how branding and creative marketing could make Charlie's line soar. But all Brady could think about was Kylie and Franny and how wrong it felt to put them out of business if they were going to franchise the business anyway. He wanted to talk to his brothers, see if it made sense to rethink the contract, but how could he show his family that they could trust him in this new endeavor when he wanted to go back on the first major thing they'd entrusted to him?

The whole thing felt like he had to choose between Kylie, the love of his life, and his family.

"So that sums up what we feel we can do for Southern Dive," Ryan said. "Do you have any immediate questions?"

The brothers looked at one another, and then Charlie and Zac both eyed Brady, because he was the finance guy, the one to figure things like this out, to ask the pertinent questions. But in his head the only question he could muster was: *Will she forgive me if I put her out of business?*

"I understand you are in the middle of an expansion?" Ryan asked. Already, Brady grew tired of the man's voice. He sounded like one of those soulless car salesmen.

"We are," Zac answered, when he realized Brady wasn't speaking up. "Really, it's been Brady's pet project, and he's done a great job fulfilling online orders in the new space. We're hoping to complete the expansion in the next few months."

Brady adjusted in his seat. "If we buy the remainder of the building."

"Why wouldn't you?" Ryan again, this time his voice filled with judgment.

"Yeah," Charlie asked. "Why wouldn't we?"

More stares, more judgment. It took everything in Brady to keep from exploding. Instead he relaxed back in his chair, the picture of control. "The contact isn't up for a few more days. We bought half the building a few months ago. The terms allow us to buy the remainder if the business that is presently there is still in jeopardy."

"And is it?" Ryan asked, and Brady's jaw ticked. Why did it seem like he was vying for information? Sure, he had vested interest in anything Southern Dive was doing now, but he didn't know Kylie or Franny. He'd never been inside Merrily. He had no right to ask about this. It was *his* thing. A family thing.

But then, if they franchised Southern Dive, it would no longer be a family thing. It would be a corporate business, and Brady promised himself he'd never do the corporate thing again. That life, that world, had turned him into the type of person he hated. A person like Ryan.

Pushing out from the table, he stood and tucked his hands into the pockets of his dress slacks. Once upon a time, he wore a suit every day. The thought felt like a distant version of the person he was today, and despite the constant drive in him to prove that he was one hundred percent invested in the family now, he didn't want to become that man again.

Which was why he couldn't simply go back on the contract. He couldn't disappoint his family again.

"Thank you for your time, Ryan. I think you've given us a lot to think about. We'll be in touch." Brady reached out to shake his hand, and immediately Ryan glanced over at Zac and Charlie.

"Um, sure. Of course. You have my contact information."

With reluctance, Zac and Charlie stood, a question mark on each of their faces, but Brady couldn't do this right now. Not when his entire life seemed to be hovering over his head, any decision able to knock it all down. He needed to think, to breathe, and he couldn't do that in a hotel's conference room.

He opened the door and stepped out to the main lobby. It was all hardwood floors and decorative rugs, and it reminded him too much of all the traveling he did back in his early days, back when he saw more hotel rooms than his own apartment.

Heading for the door, he stepped outside and drew a long breath, closing his eyes and trying to find rational thought in all the chaos in his head.

"What the hell was that?"

Sighing, Brady stared ahead at the traffic on the street in front of the hotel. A truck honked at the car in front of it. The light had turned red not seconds before, and already the driver had honked. Brady shook his head, each second causing him to become more and more aggravated.

"What was what?" he asked, his tone biting.

"You scheduled this meeting," Zac said, walking around to stand in front of him. He'd always forced his way, made you pay attention when you wanted to ignore him. Once upon a time, Brady had appreciated that about him. Right now, he wanted to tell him to stand down before he pushed him out of the way. "*You* scheduled it. After rescheduling three times. Ryan flies into town, and we leave it like that? Again, I ask, what the hell was that?"

"I don't like him."

"I repeat, you set up this meeting. If you didn't like him after the initial chat, why schedule a face-to-face?"

Brady tossed his hands. "Because I'm trying to do the best thing for you, for Charlie, for the whole damn family. And you know what I'm not thinking about? Me, or what might be best for those that I care about."

Zac tilted his head back and laughed. "I told you he wouldn't keep emotions out of it," he said to Charlie, and Brady nearly lost it.

"Right, just like you kept emotions out of it when you got involved with Sophie, who, Earth to freaking Zac, was trying to steal business from the farm!"

Zac took a step back, his eyes on the ground. "That was different."

"To hell it was. It was exactly the same. Only now, you're asking me to put my girlfriend and her godmother who just had a heart attack on the street. You think this is easy for me?"

Finally, Charlie stepped between them and placed a hand on Brady's shoulder. "Franny was going to close anyway due to her age. You know that."

"Kylie was supposed to take over."

"Did she hit her numbers?" Zac asked, forever the reasonable one of the three.

Brady raked a hand over his head. "I need to get out of here. I'll see you around."

"What are we supposed to say to Ryan?" Charlie called.

"Whatever you want," he spit back. "It's what you two want anyway, right?" He unlocked his car, jumped inside, and slammed the door, wondering when life became so complicated.

* * * *

Kylie pulled into Brady's driveway and parked, her heart heavy, the need to see him so great that she had to resist calling him as she walked up to the house.

She felt like a jerk for suggesting that he should go back on the contract, for bringing their relationship into it. At the same time...

No. She shook her head and pushed out of her car, eager to make things right with him.

A burst of cold air hit her as she stepped out into the night air, and she wished she'd thought to bring a jacket. The air smelled like fresh pines and winter, and Kylie thought of the time she and Brady walked through the woods behind his parents' house after a big snow.

As she approached the front porch, she caught lights on in the family room and a TV flashing with something Brady must be watching. He walked out from the kitchen, a beer in his hand, and Kylie drew a slow breath as she watched him sit down in his favorite recliner in front of the TV. Her chest constricted. God, she loved him. A part of her wondered if she'd ever stopped.

She thought of him agreeing to split the shop. Him coming to the hospital after Franny's heart attack. Him standing in line at Target at four in the morning for Rena's doll.

Brady wasn't just a good man. He was a great man. And she needed to give him an opportunity to do the right thing by Franny.

Reaching for the doorbell, she pressed it once, then took a step back and wrapped her arms around her body to try to warm herself.

A few seconds passed, then a minute, and worry set in. Trying again, Kylie pressed the doorbell once more, then stepped back again.

Finally, she heard footsteps from inside, followed by the door being unlocked. The door opened slowly, and Kylie grinned up at Brady, but he didn't grin back.

"Hey, what are you doing here?" he asked.

Okay, not the reception she was hoping for.

"Um, I was hoping we could talk."

He glanced inside, then back at her. "Did you call? I didn't notice a text or missed call on my phone."

"No. I hoped we could talk in person." She shivered, whether from the cold outside or Brady's cold greeting, she couldn't be sure. "Can I come inside?"

"Yeah, sure," he said, running a hand over his head. He backed up and waved for her to come in. Clearly, she should have thought through the whole just-showing-up thing.

Stepping inside, Kylie caught the definitive smell of delivery pizza, and that nervous feeling in her rose up again. He was eating dinner, which meant he'd been back from the meeting with the investor for some time now. Why hadn't he called her?

"Are you eating dinner? I wasn't trying to interrupt anything."

Brady crossed his arms and stared at her. "You're not. What's up?"

What's up?

"I..." What the heck happened to the Brady she saw earlier that day? Maybe she should have texted him that she was sorry earlier.

"I was hoping to talk about the contract."

He shut his eyes and sighed heavily. "Of course you want to talk about the contract."

"I just—"

"You're just thinking of you and your family. What about my family, huh?" he asked, his voice growing louder. "What about the fact that they're counting on me to do what I agreed to do—which is honoring this contract? How about the fact that we need that building or the fact that Southern Dive sells about three times as much as Merrily even in your best month? But none of that matters, right?"

"I didn't say that. Actually, I was coming to say—"

"Let me guess? That I'm a giant dick, right? That I only care about money and success and that I'd screw over anyone, even someone I care about for the right deal?"

"No, that's not—"

"Because you're right, in a way. I guess that was the person I was before, and maybe I deserve this shit now. But I was trying here. I was trying to keep what we are separate from all the rest. But you can't ask me to choose you over my family. You can't and I won't." He crossed his arms and stared at her, and Kylie wondered if she'd stepped into some nightmare or something. Surely, this wasn't really happening.

It felt so much like the fight they'd had all those years ago—her trying to talk to him and understand, him shutting her down completely. Well, screw that.

"You know, I came here to talk to you, but—"

"No, you came here to convince me to do what you wanted me to do."

And that did it. "You know what? Screw this and screw you. You haven't allowed me to say anything at all, and maybe if you had, you'd see that you're wrong about me. But you have never given me a chance, have you? It's always you and your thoughts and they can't possibly be wrong, right? Well, I'm done with that. I've spent my entire life wondering if I screwed this up." She motioned between them. "But it's crystal clear to me that it was never me. It's one hundred percent you and your ego. So you can take your ego and the building and whatever the hell else you want, but I'm out."

She started for the door, when he called after her. "Yeah, run away, Ky. Like always."

The bitterness in his voice cut through her, and tears pricked her eyes, but she refused to cry in front of him. She straightened and reached for the doorknob. "Good-bye, Brady."

Cold air hit her again, but this time she didn't feel it. Anger and sadness swirled in her chest, each fighting it out for control. How could he say those things? How could he even think those things? He hadn't given her a chance to explain, to make things right. But then maybe this was all for the best. If Brady cared so little about her that he could turn her away at something like this, how would they ever survive real-world problems? When finances came into it, and kids and whatever?

They wouldn't. Because Brady would always view success above everything else.

Which meant they were never meant to be.

Kylie slipped into her car and put it in reverse. She made it as far as the end of the driveway before her tears spilled down her cheeks.

It was over, but then, maybe they'd never been in the first place.

Chapter 21

"You look like shit."

Brady glanced up from his desk in the back of ETC. He'd brought the desk in the day after Kylie left his house, her taillights shining out in his head long after she'd disappeared into the night. And then, because he couldn't simply hang out across from her knowing she didn't want to be with him, he hired a full-time sales person to manage the front.

But that didn't prevent his brothers from coming over to talk to him in his quiet space in the back corner of the stockroom, or Ally from standing over him with a disconcerting look on her face.

"Come again?" he said, even though he knew exactly what she'd said.

"I said you look like shit."

His eyebrows lifted. "That's what I thought you said, but I wanted to see if you'd go there twice."

"Do you want me to say it a third time just to drive home the point?"

With a sigh, he leaned back in his chair and set down his pen. He'd been poring over December numbers, reconciling everything both Southern Dive & ETC did for the month, because he was too much of a hands-on person to hire a bookkeeper.

"What can I do for you, Ally?"

She glanced behind her, then rose onto her toes to look around the stockroom. "You can get your head out of your ass, that's what you can do."

For the second time, his eyebrows rose. "Did I put a box in the wrong place or something?"

Exasperated, Ally grabbed his arm and tugged until he stood up. "What are you doing—where are we—why are you dragging me away from my desk?"

"Shhh." She pulled his arm until they stood by the door to the inside, and then quietly pushed it open, peeked through the crack, then beckoned Brady to do the same. "You see that? You did that, and I need you to fix it."

Through the door's crack, they had a clear view of Kylie behind Merrily's counter, her shoulders hunched, her hair tied back in a messy bun, not a stitch of makeup on her face. In place of her usual, semi-put together look, she wore an oversized sweatshirt and leggings. His heart clenched at the sight of her, but though he knew Ally was trying to drive home the point that Kylie was a mess, all Brady could see was the most beautiful person he'd ever seen in his life. And how real it was that she was no longer his.

"I don't know what you want me to see here."

"She's a disaster, and you're a disaster. Together you're one big, giant disaster. And you know she doesn't have the confidence to fix it. She's already convinced herself that you've moved on and likely never wanted her in the first place."

"She what?"

"I know, right? Girl's gone crazy."

Brady was a stubborn man, but surely he'd made it clear to her how much he cared about her. Surely she realized that he was aching as badly as she was, but then, he wasn't the one to walk away. She left, not him.

"You don't seem to understand. I didn't end this. She did. It's not me that can put it back together, because I didn't quit."

Ally leaned back and planted a hand on her hip, her head doing that swivel thing that said he better back up and deliver a different story. "You think I don't know exactly what went down at your house, Mister? 'Cause I do. She goes there to apologize for even mentioning the contract, to tell you that she was shouldn't have gone there. And you shut her down, went off on her. Made her feel like she shouldn't have even been at your house. Is that not the truth?"

"Well..." Not the whole truth, anyway. "I had a bad day. Have you ever had a bad day? A day when maybe you weren't the nicest to your husband, to your daughter? A day when you needed to be able to think things out and you couldn't be left alone enough to do it?"

"Nah, God made me perfect."

Brady stared at her.

"Fine, maybe. But see, the difference is that I know when to say I'm sorry. Why can't you say you're sorry?"

"You aren't listening. She left me. She said it was over."

"You told her that she was making you choose between her and your family. I mean, seriously? What a stupid, childish thing to say."

All right, so maybe that was going too far. "You don't understand."

Ally crossed her arms. "Then enlighten me."

The door closed back, and Brady walked away, needing some space so he could find the right words. "I used to be a big corporate guy. The kind who thought the most important thing in the world was the next sale. Then one day I'm at the biggest convention of the year for my firm, out with all the bigwigs, and I get a call from my mom. Then my brother. Then my sister. Then my other brother. I ignored all of them. Finally, they sent me a text and said it was an emergency, to call them." Brady shook his head as the memory hit him, followed immediately by his reaction to the text. "I turned off my phone. My dad had a heart attack, was taken into emergency surgery, and I turned off my freaking phone."

"You didn't know," Ally said. "I'm sure they understood. You were at a convention."

"I spent years putting work, myself, anything I could come up with before my family. And the sad thing? They expected it. I finally returned their call and grabbed a red eye home, only to get there and find out that they never expected me to come in the first place. My dad fought like a warrior through the night, and when he woke from surgery the next day and we learned that he could no longer manage the farm, I promised my family that I would be there. I would never let them down again. It took me years to prove to them that I was serious about that promise. I quit my job in New York, moved back home, and worked the farm, until my brothers and I decided to open Southern Dive. It's been a grind every day, but I do it, because they deserve for me to be there for them."

Ally leaned against the wall beside the door. "You can do the right thing by Franny and Kylie and still do the right thing by your family."

"Oh, yeah, how? Honestly, I'm all ears. Please, tell me something that would make both sides equally happy."

At that, Ally bit her lip. "Okay, so I didn't really mean that I knew what you should do. I just meant that you're a smart, capable guy. Surely you can come up with something."

"The contract is air tight. Zac and Charlie would have conceded losing half the business, but they won't go back on our agreement. The only fix is if Merrily can sell the three thousand needed. Do you see that happening in the next couple of days?"

Just then, Kylie pushed through the door and stopped cold. Her eyes met Brady, and without thinking, he pushed off the table he'd been leaning against and took a step toward her.

"Hey," she said, her voice so unlike the cheerful one he knew that it broke his heart.

"Hey."

He tried to draw a breath, but couldn't quite get his lungs to work properly. How could he stand this close to someone who owned such a giant piece of his heart, his soul, and still feel this distant from her?

"Kylie, can we—"

The moment her eyes left his, he knew she was gone. Her attention fell on Ally, and he could swear that her bottom lip was shaking.

"Al, can you come help me up front, please?"

Ally's face fell, and Brady feared what she was seeing on Kylie's face that Kylie didn't show to him. Hurt and disappointment and pain and probably more emotions than he could possibly process, all of them by his hand.

The guilt was too much.

"Sure, honey. I'm right behind you."

Kylie headed back through the door she'd just come through, without whatever she'd come there to get, all so she could get away from Brady. That was where they were.

"Fix this," Ally growled and pointed at him. "Now. I will not see that sweet girl that miserable another day. Fix it."

If only he knew how to without destroying his family's trust in the process.

* * * *

"I'm in here," Franny called as Kylie set down her keys on the kitchen counter, each move harder, each breath harder.

There should be some kind of free pass from seeing your ex after he dumped you. Like a universal rule that God would make him go left when you went right, so your heart could recover. But no. Instead, she'd walked into the stupid stockroom and saw Brady and then she did the stupidest thing of all—she locked up, full stare and all. But he was standing *right* there, mere feet away, dressed in her favorite look on him—flannel shirt and jeans—with just the right amount of scruff on his face, and she couldn't seem to make her stupid limbs walk.

Clearly, she was riddled with stupid these days. That was the only explanation for her getting involved with a man who had destroyed her heart as a teen and thinking there would be any other outcome this time.

"You look like crap," Franny said.

"I don't." Reflexively, Kylie reached up to adjust her hair, then dropped her arm back at her side. "Ah, who am I kidding? I do. I can't help it."

"Honey, just go talk to him."

The sadness that Kylie fought off like an evil spirit crept back up. "See, that's the thing, Fran. I did go talk to him. He shut me down, told me that

I was making him choose between his family and me. I would never do that. I love his family. It would kill me to hurt them."

"But don't you see? Asking him to rethink the contact was asking him to choose."

"Yeah, but—"

"No, buts. It was. You didn't mean any harm by it. Sweet girl, sometimes I think you love me too much. But I am your past." Kylie opened her mouth to argue, but Franny threw up her hand to stop her. "I am. He is your future. You have to be willing to stay. You can't always run when things get bad. Men can be pigheaded and selfish. But, news flash: so can women. Marriage is about compromise and pushing through all the bad stuff, because it's worth it when you get to the good stuff."

Franny stood up to come over to Kylie, but immediately grimaced and gripped her chest.

"Are you okay?" Kylie asked.

Franny rubbed the spot on her chest and continued on toward Kylie. "Yeah, just a little heartburn."

"Um, no. You had a heart attack not a month ago. We promised your doctor if you had any issues we would call."

"I'm fine," Franny said, waving it off, but Kylie wasn't willing to take the chance.

"Sit back down. I'm calling your doctor." She took out her phone and dialed Franny's cardiologist, who instructed them to go to the hospital.

Franny rubbed the spot on her chest again, and Kylie grabbed her keys. "I'm taking her there right now," she said into the phone, then hung up and eyed her godmother. "All right, Ms. Heartburn. Let's get you to the car. We're going to the ER."

"Kylie Anne, I am perfectly fine."

Tears burned Kylie's eyes as she walked over to Franny and kneeled down beside her. "Listen, I know you know your own body. I realize this could very well be nothing, but I'm not asking you, I'm begging you. Please, humor me. Please. I can't take losing you, too."

Reaching up to cup her cheek, Franny kissed her forehead and pushed to standing. "All right, but I get to make a call on the way."

Kylie helped Franny put on her shoes, grabbed her purse, then helped her into the car. She passed over Franny's phone, her thoughts inward as she silently prayed that this was nothing. The other possibility was too much to bear.

Chapter 22

Brady parked outside his parents' house, not really sure when he decided to go there, but feeling a bit better already. His mom and dad had a way about them that made the complicated seem easy. Hopefully they could shed some light on his current situation before he lost his mind.

"Y'all here?" he called as he walked on inside, not bothering to knock. The door was always unlocked.

"Out back," a deep voice called, and Brady followed the path of fishing gear from the foyer, through the family room, and out to the back patio. His dad stood beside a dozen or so poles, with another one in his hand.

"What are you doing? Selling everything you have?"

His father glanced up, then back to the pole. "Cleaning them to gear up for the season."

Brady eyed his father. "You never hit the lake before March."

"Can never plan too early. But something tells me you aren't here to talk about fishing."

The temperature was warm outside for January. So warm that even at night the temperature couldn't be lower than fifty. It seemed like an eternity ago that he and Kylie were standing in the snow outside the movie theater, a wealth of possibilities before them. How had they gotten here?

"Why are you cleaning them outside at night?"

"Your mama doesn't like the smell inside the house, and I was bored, so here I am."

"Where is she?"

"Visiting Kate, but she should be back soon. Now, your turn."

Brady released a slow breath and sat down at the patio table, a mess of fishing rods all around him. Strewn across the table was reel after reel and tackle box after tackle box. "You ever feel like any way you turn is the wrong way?"

Dad's brows pulled together. "Like when you're driving?"

"No, like..." Brady shook his head and decided to try again. "Have you ever felt like you were making a decision that could impact the rest of your life?"

He set down the pole in his hand and pulled out the chair across from Brady. "Why don't you say what's on your mind, son? Then we can get to the part where I tell you it's all going to be okay. Because it will be okay. No matter what it is, in the end, it will all be okay."

"Not this."

His father threaded his fingers together and rested his hands against the table. "Let me be the decider of that. What happened?"

Brady thought of his father in the hospital after the heart attack, how small he'd looked. Maybe that was why he felt such a pull to help Franny. He saw how it weakened his dad and knew firsthand how hard it was to help a person through the realization that he could no longer be the person he was before.

He drew a shallow breath and released, that ache in his chest building and making it hard to breathe fully. "You know that Zac, Charlie, and I signed the contract with Franny to buy half of her building, right?"

"I do," Dad said. "Go on."

"Well, in the contract, it states that Merrily had to hit a certain sales quota for December in order to keep the other half of the business. If they did it, then they'd keep their half and we'd keep ours. We never really worked through what that would mean, because none of us honestly thought it would happen."

"And what happens if Merrily didn't hit its numbers?"

"They sell the other half to us at half its value."

His father's eyes widened, clear disappointment on his face. "Those terms seem a bit unfair."

"Yeah. Well, it gets worse. Merrily is three thousand short of hitting the quota needed to keep their half of the business. Kylie asked for an extra week to hit the goal."

"And you told her no."

Brady's glanced up from where he'd been staring at the table, too ashamed to meet his father's eyes. "How did you know?"

"Because you've been trying to prove that you are family-first since my heart attack. But that was years ago, son. You can't spend the rest of your life saying you were sorry. I was never upset at you."

"You should have been."

He laughed. "If a near life-threatening experience teaches you anything, it's that the trivial things don't matter and holding grudges are a waste of energy."

"Maybe. But it doesn't change the fact that Zac and Charlie are expecting me to maintain the terms of the contract and to move forward with the investor."

"What do you think?"

Brady leaned back in his chair and stared up at the stars above. The sounds of night surrounded them, quiet except for the wind in the trees. "I think I'm choosing between my family and…the love of my life."

His dad laughed again, this time harder.

"What?"

"Son, there is no choice there."

"I know, family is—"

"You choose the love of your life."

Brady's gaze snapped back to his dad. "What?"

"You choose the love of your life," his dad said leaning forward again. "Look, I know we've taught y'all that family comes first, but you have to understand, for us, that's this family. Mom, you kids. That's my family, and I put you above anyone else. You can't have that version of family if you don't put that love of your life above everything else. If you can't make her your center and build your life around what you have together. That is living. And that is exactly what Zac and Charlie and Kate have all done. Why not you?"

"But the contract says that Merrily had to hit three thousand more in sales, and they only have two more days. They won't sell three thousand in two days."

A glint sparked in his dad's eyes. "Unless you help them."

Brady's face scrunched in confusion, and then realization overcame him. "Unless I help them."

His father checked his watch. "They have a website, right?"

Brady nodded. "Yeah, yeah they do." He pushed to standing and started for the door.

"Where you going?"

He smiled. "To do some shopping."

Chapter 23

Kylie stretched a slice of thick tape across the bottom of the corrugated box, then another on the ends. She flipped the box right and opened up the top, then layered in bubble wrap. Then she passed the box over to Ally, who filled the box and then passed it to Franny.

Thankfully, Franny had been right about having heartburn two nights ago, so she was able to come back home. Still, it had taken a lot for Kylie to agree to let her come close up the shop. A part of her wanted to push Franny on it, sacrifice the hurt of seeing her baby close by staying at home. But Franny told her that she opened the shop on its first day. It didn't seem right for anyone else to close it.

And so, with heavy hearts she, Franny, and Ally met at the shop to box up the last of the online orders before they started the difficult task of cleaning out the shop for good.

"Have you noticed an uptick of orders this week?" Ally asked as she filled the box with the next order, double checked the packing slip, then passed it off to Franny.

Kylie lifted her shoulder in a half shrug. "Maybe. I haven't been paying that much attention. Online orders were never enough of our business for it to make a difference."

"Expensive stuff, too," Ally said, ignoring Kylie's negative mood. She and Franny had been doing that a lot this week. "I mean, who honestly buys a two-hundred-dollar porcelain Santa?"

Kylie reached for the order. "Apparently, Apple Bigton."

"Apple Bigton?" Ally said, laughing. "The last one was Pear Bigton."

"No," Kylie said, covering her mouth to hide her grin. "Sisters? Surely, parents don't name their kids such atrocious names, right?"

"Clearly, they do. And it doesn't stop there. Check this out." Ally passed her latest order over to Kylie. "Clementine."

"Bigton? Let me see that."

Sure enough, the name Clementine Bigton, followed by a P.O. box number. The P.O. box was different from the other two, but all of the orders listed Williamstown, Kentucky, as the city and state. Williamstown was a small town not fifteen minutes away, and though Kylie hadn't been there often, she thought she would remember a family of sisters with fruit names.

"Do you know them, Fran?" Ally asked.

Franny shook her head. "Honey, I can barely remember you two."

The women all laughed and went back to their work, but Kylie couldn't shake the feeling that she was missing something.

"Wow, this order is for nearly six hundred dollars. Are these sisters starting their own holiday shop and buying up your stuff to do it?"

The thought rubbed Kylie the wrong way. "No, I'm sure they're just fans of Christmas collectibles." She taped another box and passed it to Ally.

"Right. Do you see this stack of boxes?"

Kylie glanced over at the shipping table that Brady had allowed them to use for packing. It was covered in packages. "All of them are for the sisters?"

"All except two, which are going to…" She checked the list. "Green Farmer."

"You're joking," Kylie deadpanned. "That is not the name."

"It is. See for yourself." Once again, she handed the list over to Kylie, who scanned down to see the names.

Apple Bigton
Pear Bigton
Clementine Bigton
Green Farmer

"Do you have a list of yesterday's shipments?" she asked Ally.

"Yeah, right here." Ally walked around to her desk, opened a drawer, and returned with a stapled report.

Kylie read the names on the list, each one causing her anger to spark more and more. In addition to the names from today, there were three others.

Summer Farmer
Mr. Bate Casting
Mrs. Cot Abigun

All of the addresses listed a P.O. box in Williamstown. Maybe Ally was onto something after all.

"Is there a way to get more information on who manages a P.O. box?" she asked the other two women, who merely shook their heads. "But surely someone at the post office would remember the person, right? Think of your P.O. box, Franny. Everyone at the post office knows you. Maybe someone there would remember the person."

"People, you mean," Ally said. "There's like seven people here."

Kylie's face pulled into a knowing smile. "Or there's just one person, pretending to be seven, so she can use our stuff to start her own business."

"Well, even if that were the case, what does it matter? We can't hit our goal." Ally dropped another shipment into its box, a somber expression on her face.

"But what if we could hit our goal?"

Kylie and Ally spun around to find Franny staring down at her phone.

"What do you mean?" Kylie asked.

"Look at this," Franny said, passing her phone to Kylie. "It's an email from our accountant with an updated monthly sales total for December. We're at $16,500. We're only five hundred dollars from the goal now."

"It can't be. I checked that number just three days ago and we were still more than two thousand off. There's barely been anyone in the store since Christmas. So how…" She spun around to look at the pile of packages on the shipping table.

"I told you we've been slammed online. I knew I didn't have all these stupid cuts on my hands for nothing." Ally held up her palms to show several cuts from packaging up the shipments. "Someone's become a fan of our site!"

"I don't know," Kylie said, eyeing the list of names again. "Something's fishy here."

"Maybe it's Mr. Lg Fish," Ally said giggling.

"See, that has to be a fake name, right? No one is named Mr. Lg Fish. Or Mr. Green Farmer. I mean, seriously. Those are not real names."

Ally cocked her head. "I don't know. Celebrities name their kids all kinds of weird crap."

"Yeah and how many celebrities do you see running around Crestler's Key? Or Williamstown, for that matter. Is there even a stoplight there?"

"No clue," Ally said. "But how would you find out? It's a P.O. box. You can't just Google Maps this person."

"No," Kylie said, grabbing her purse. "But I can drive over there and ask the post office staff if they know any of the names."

"You aren't serious." Ally set down the box she was packing.

Franny walked around to where Kylie stood and took her hand. "Sweetie, I think it's time you let this place go." The sadness in her voice cemented Kylie's resolve all the more.

"I will if it comes to that. I promise. But we are five hundred dollars away from keeping the store running. Don't you at least want to know how that happened?"

A ping came from the laptop on Ally's desk, and she walked over, clicked a few things, then peered back over at Kylie and Franny with new excitement. "Scratch that. We just hit our goal."

"What? No way." Kylie's heartbeat picked up, new energy swirling around in her chest.

"We just received another order for just over five hundred dollars."

Kylie's eyebrows pulled together. "Let me see that." She wandered over to the laptop and opened the order. It was for a full Christmas village, complete with people and a running train. Franny said they'd had the village for years, no one willing to buy the whole thing, and Franny couldn't imagine selling it piece by piece. Someone had bought it. Someone named...

"You have got to be freaking kidding me."

"What is it?" Ally asked. "Fake order?"

"You tell me." Kylie pointed at the name Mr. S. Diving. "S. Diving. Seriously? That is not a person's name."

"Hold on a second," Franny said walking over to join the other two women. "S. Diving? Like scuba diving?"

Ally clicked the other again and scrolled down. "There isn't a first name listed anywhere on the order. Only the 'S.'"

"And what were the other names again?" Franny asked. Kylie handed her godmother the two reports and watched as a slow smile spread across Franny's face. "I'll be damned."

"What?" Ally and Kylie asked together.

"I think I know who your buyer is, and I agree that it's one person. But not a woman."

"A man? But who—"

Kylie scrolled to the bottom of the order again.

S. Diver
Green Farmer
Summer Farmer
Lg. Fish
Cot. Abigun
Apple Bigton
Pear Bigton
Clementine Bigton
Apples, pears, clementines—all fruit grown at...
"Oh my God," Ally said.

"I think I know where you need to go," Franny added, her face beaming with joy.

Kylie took the report from Franny and raced for the door. "Already there. Wish me luck."

"Good luck!" they called.

Chapter 24

Kylie rushed up Brady's front steps and slammed to a halt. What was she doing there? What was her plan? She couldn't exactly knock on his door and order him to confess everything. He'd look at her like she was insane. And then, what if she was wrong? There could be a Mr. Green Farmer out there in the world, even in Williamstown, where he lived with his wife, who loved Christmas stuff, so he ordered things from Merrily to surprise her. And maybe her name was Summer Farmer, which made perfect sense, come to think of it. Green and Summer Farmer.

Lord. She covered her face with her hands and laughed. There was so not a Green and Summer Farmer! But that didn't mean that Brady was involved with this—

"Ky?"

Crap! And now in her mind's crazy psychobabble she'd missed him opening the door.

Slowly, Kylie peeled away her hands from her face and stared up at Brady Littleton. Today he wore jeans and a basic white tee, and damn if it wasn't the best thing she'd ever seen on a man. She stared at him, curious how to have this conversation, when his eyebrows lifted and he asked, "Are you okay?"

"Yes. Great, actually. You?"

He peered around, like he was searching for something behind her, then looked back at her. "Fine."

"Good." She nodded along with the word like a complete freaking moron. *Speak, woman, speak!*

"So..."

"So." She smiled this time. *Just ask him. Ask!*

"Was there something that you—"

"Are you Green Farmer?"

Brady's head cocked, his eyebrows threading together. "Come again?"

And now was the time that a sane woman would take a step back, laugh off the intrusion, and run for her car, but see, the problem with that plan was that Kylie was tired of running. She wanted to stand still, fearless and free, and there was no getting to fearless and free without taking some risks from time to time.

So, with that new confidence, she pressed on, this time slower so he could hear her clearly. "I asked if you were Green Farmer. Or maybe Cot Abigun? Or Apple Bigton?"

He scrubbed a hand over her jaw and stared at her. "Big ton?"

Kylie waved her hands in a circular, hurry-up-and-get-this fashion. "You know, Bigton. Like Littleton, but instead of little you insert big. Bigton."

Brady tucked his hands into his pockets. His stare was still in place, but it had morphed from surprise at seeing her to confusion to now something that resembled pity. Oh God, she was wrong. He wasn't Green Farmer, and she'd come all the way out here, prepared to throw her heart on the line, and he wasn't any of those people. This was all just a giant misunderstanding.

"Right. I must be confused. I'm sorry I bothered you." She took a step back and dropped her head.

"Kylie, are you okay?"

Without looking back at him, she shook her head. "No...I'm not." She started around the sidewalk, her pride a ghost of what it'd once been, when she heard the mailman's truck driving up Brady's driveway. The mailman parked behind Kylie's car, stepped out, grabbed two large boxes, and made his way over to the front porch.

Kylie squinted at the boxes as he neared, until she caught the side of the box, and the swirly, happy logo that she would recognize anywhere.

Merrily Christmas.

Spinning on her heels, she rushed up the steps and pushed past Brady, ignoring his calls and questions of where she was going. She couldn't answer him, could scarcely think. All she could do was focus on the task before her.

Kylie scanned his foyer, then his office, then his dining room, all to come up empty. They had to be here somewhere, but where? She walked around his kitchen, with no signs of boxes, then went back to his bedroom. Again, nothing.

"Ky, what are you—"

"*Shh*. They're somewhere. I just need to think ..." She snapped her fingers, the memory of Brady talking about his finished basement coming back to her, and how he didn't have anything to put down there.

Rounding out of his master bedroom, she grabbed the door to his basement and swung it open, Brady on her heels.

"What are you doing? Don't go down there—It's not clean—finished, I mean. Don't—"

Kylie jumped down the final two steps and flicked on the lights, only to stumble back, her heart in her throat as she took in the open common room and package after package after package. There were too many to count, too many to process, each unopened, but she didn't need to know what was inside. The Merrily logo stared back at her from all the boxes, a confirmation of what she'd suspected back at the shop and what she should have known about Brady all along.

Tears spilled down her cheeks as she turned around, and for the first time in her life, she was at a loss for words.

"Now, listen, I know how this looks," Brady said. "I just wanted to..." He threw a hand out toward the packages and then shook his head slowly.

Kylie started for him, each step like coming closer to home. "You're Green Farmer."

Brady ran his thumb over her cheek to catch a fallen tear. "I'm Green Farmer."

"But why?"

"Because I love you. Always have, always will."

And that did it. Kylie surged forward, her arms wrapping around his neck as her lips came up to meet his. She kissed him for the days they'd spent apart this week and all the days they'd spent apart before, when they were still trying to find their way back to one another. Finally, she pulled back and looked him in the eye and said the words she'd longed to say for too long: "I love you, too. So much."

Brady cradled her face with his hands and pressed another kiss to her lips, and Kylie thought finally, she would have her happily ever after. Until the sound of a man clearing his throat from behind them had them separating.

"I'm sorry to disturb you," the mailman said, a sheepish expression on his face. "But you didn't say where you wanted me to leave this when you asked me to leave it inside. Plus, I have three more boxes."

A grin split Kylie's face. "Three more boxes?"

Brady cocked his head. "I might have gone a little overboard."

"You think?"

"What can I say? I'm a little obsessed with the manager." He kissed her cheek, then her neck, and pulled her closer.

"So the contract?" she asked, feeling uneasy again.

"Is void. You met your sales goal, we keep half, you keep half."

"Brady, I can't let you do this. You've spent a fortune." Kylie eyed the boxes again as the mailman brought around the other boxes and set them with the stacks in front of them.

"You can and you will. It's just money. I don't need it. What I need is you, and I couldn't live with myself if I caused Merrily to shut down."

The mailman brought around another box, and then waved good-bye, leaving Brady and Kylie alone again. She smiled up at him, relief hitting her. "So we're partners again?"

Brady pulled her to him, his eyes on hers. "Partners for life, if you'll agree to put up with me that long. I'm yours for as long as you'll let me stay."

Kylie rose onto her toes and kissed him again. "How about forever?"

Brady hugged her close. "Forever sounds perfect."

Epilogue

Ten months later

"I'll take a large—no, maybe a medium. Do they shrink?"

Kylie beamed at the woman before her counter, the woman's focus on the wall of T-shirts behind her, and the bubbly feeling inside Kylie soared. "They're preshrunk, so I think you can do a medium."

The woman placed a finger on her lips in thought. She had golden-tanned skin and short blond hair. Her two kids played in Merrily's kid center while their mama shopped. "I'll take the yellow and turquoise. No, white and yellow. No, white and turquoise. Oh…how do you not buy them all?" she asked Kylie, who laughed.

"I have every design at home, long-sleeve and short-sleeve. They're addictive."

The woman shot Kylie a pained expression, and Kylie decided on a new bulk sale for the T-shirts. "How about if you buy two you get one for half price?"

"You would do that?" the woman asked, already pulling out her wallet like she was afraid Kylie would change her mind.

"Absolutely."

"Yay! Okay, I'll take the white, yellow, and turquoise, and then these." The woman placed a set of candles on the counter, and Kylie's grin spread.

When Charlie first came to her about designing shirts for the new business, she'd been hesitant. What if no one wanted one? But then she saw the designs, each new one more adorable than the last, and she was sold.

It had been scary to add a new product after the expansion from Christmas to home goods, but then Charlie showed her the uptick in sales for Southern Dive when he added the shirts, and she decided to trust her soon-to-be brother-in-law.

Wow. Brother-in-law.

The butterfly feeling in her stomach flittered back to life. It was always there, right below the surface, but she tried to keep it under control at the shop, otherwise—

"Good God, are you ever going to stop smiling like a fool?" Ally asked as she wrapped up the T-shirts.

"Oh! Are you engaged?" the woman asked, reaching for Kylie's hand.

"I am!" Again, Kylie beamed like a fool, and Ally rolled her eyes.

"You know, you're the one who told me I'd be crazy not to marry him."

Ally finished bagging the purchase and passed it over to the customer. "I still say that. The man's hot as sin," she said to the woman, causing her to laugh.

"Do you have a picture?" she asked.

"I do."

Kylie bent down to grab her phone from where she'd tucked it under the counter, when a voice said, "Or you could just introduce him."

Kylie jumped to her feet, her heartbeat picking up speed as a slow smile spread across her face. "I thought you would be in Atlanta for another week."

Brady started for her. "What can I say? I left something pretty important at home, and I couldn't function right without her." He stopped in front of her, ignoring the stares of all the women in the shop.

"Wow, he is hot," the customer said.

"See, I told you." Ally propped her elbow up on the counter. "The whole family's like that. It's ridiculous."

A laugh broke from Brady, but he didn't pull his eyes away from Kylie. It had been over a week since she'd seen him, and while it was hard, Kylie knew that he would come back to her.

Southern Dive's franchising had taken a lot of effort from all the brothers, but each new city brought on more success and security for the family, and Kylie couldn't be happier for them.

"Miss me?" Brady asked, coming in closer. He brought his mouth down to hers, kissing her lightly, but after a week, that wasn't going to get it done.

"Come with me." She took his hand, earning a fresh eye roll from Ally.

"They're going to get it on in the back," Ally said to the customer.

"Ally!" Kylie scolded, but Brady only winked in reply.

Kylie pushed through the swinging door, not bothering to see if anyone was in the back, and spun around, her arms snaking around his neck and her lips crashing against his before he could say a word.

His tongue slipped into her mouth as he pulled her closer, and Kylie thought, *Now, this? This is happiness.*

Brady leaned away from her and chuckled. "Don't look so disappointed. I came bearing gifts."

That perked her up. Brady had brought her something back from each of the cities he'd traveled to for Southern Dive's expansion. Some were ornaments for their tree, others were keepsakes that could only be found in that town or city.

"Stay here and close your eyes. It's in my car."

Kylie smiled at him, but obeyed. She closed her eyes and listened as he opened the back door. A minute or two passed, then the door opened again, and she heard him near.

"Okay, open."

She opened her eyes, and immediately covered her mouth with her hands. "Is that…?"

Brady held out the bright red bag to her, a star and the words AMERICAN GIRL printed on the outside. "Early Christmas present. Open it."

Beaming, Kylie set down the bag on a packing table near them and slipped out a long, rectangular box. She slipped the top of the box off, and there were no words. Tears pricked her eyes as she took in the doll—light skin, brown curly hair, brown eyes. A handful of freckles dotted her nose.

It looked exactly like her.

"You bought me an American Girl doll." All the memories of her asking for one for Christmas and her parents never buying it came rushing to the surface. All the sadness, all the disappointment. And Brady had bought her one.

"I know it's not that Samantha doll you wanted when you were little, but there's an American Girl store in Atlanta, and they have these 'Truly Me' dolls, and I thought maybe you wouldn't want a doll that would remind you of what you didn't have as a little girl. Maybe you would want one that reminded you that you're with me? You will always have what you need. I will never let you down."

Her tears slipped down her cheeks as she set the doll back on the table and wrapped her arms around him. "I love you so much."

"I love you, too," Brady said, kissing her. "And I can't wait to spend the rest of my life with you."

ABOUT THE AUTHOR

USA Today bestselling author **Melissa West** is the author of more than fifteen novels, each set in the South and ready to steal a reader's heart with Southern charm, sweet tea, and a whole mess of gossip. Her novels have received high praise and recognition from *RT Book Reviews*, *Seventeen Magazine*, Fresh Fiction, and Harlequin Junkie, among others.

When not writing, she enjoys spending time with her family in Georgia.

MELISSA WEST

CHASING LOVE

THE LITTLETON BROTHERS

MELISSA WEST

FIGHTING LOVE

THE LITTLETON BROTHERS

Printed in the United States
by Baker & Taylor Publisher Services